THE DEPUTY'S MISSION

MARIA MICHAELS

To all those who believe no sin is too great to be forgiven.

Chapter 1

Vera Carrington shifted gears and ramped up her speed, grateful for the car's get up and go. Fortunately, the roads had already been cleared from last night's snowfall. She had assigned herself the early shift at her café, but the darkness of the January morning had done nothing to wake her.

Her regular customers at The Bean expected the doors to open at six. She had about an hour's worth of preparations she'd have to accomplish in about fifteen minutes.

Times were tough in their resort town, now. Fewer tourists and vacationers were making the trek to the California Sierra mountain town.

The wail of a siren split the air and in her rearview mirror, the police lights flashed.

Not again. The third speeding ticket she'd have to talk her way out of in as many months? This was the last thing she needed. Especially now. She was already two months behind on her home's mortgage payment and still had no idea what to do.

She couldn't afford this ticket. Maybe she could talk her way out of it just one more time. After that, she'd start paying better attention to the speedometer.

She pulled over near a six-foot-high snow embankment and watched in the rearview mirror as Ryan Colton climbed out of the cruiser. She sighed. Ryan was different since he'd caught religion and become a regular at Jack and Maggie's church. Talking her way out of this one wouldn't be easy.

"Hi there, Ryan." Vera hit the button and let some of the cold morning air seep through the now opened window.

A pang of guilt stabbed her. The right thing to do would be to take her punishment. She could hear Maggie's voice echoing in the recesses of her mind.

"You're my best friend, but I'm married to the sheriff now. Behave yourself."

"Hey, Vera. Do you have any idea how fast you were going?" Ryan had his flashlight out but avoided shining it in her eyes.

"I'm sorry about that. Hit the snooze too many times. I overslept."

He took out his ticket pad, expertly balancing his flashlight. "I know what that's like."

"I'm not a morning person and I would assign the shift to Annie, but I can't afford the payroll right now." Maybe with his new-found religion, Ryan might have a little compassion for a hard working girl. "Especially with Maggie on maternity leave. You know, Jack's wife?"

"You wouldn't be trying to talk me out of writing this ticket, would you?" He was clean cut now, having shaved off his beard a few months ago, though it didn't take away from his rugged good looks. He'd always been difficult to ignore and now he was so darned *nice*.

"Who, me?" Vera tossed her hair back and hoped she wasn't too obvious. Ryan was not as gullible as the younger officers.

"Because I do recall the last time I let you go I reminded you it would be the last time." He flashed that disarming and cocky grin.

Stop it; stop smiling at me like that.

"I do remember that." She tried not to melt under his penetrating stare. His expressive brown eyes had a way of untangling her frayed nerves.

"I would let it go, but Jack had a talk with us. He says you've got to learn your lesson."

"I have a reputation, I see." Vera tapped her red fingernail on the steering wheel.

"For speeding. Yes, you do."

Vera stepped out of the car hoping she might have a better effect, get him to step back, and take a look.

He stood his ground.

She considered flirting with him. Not only would it be effective, but it might also be fun. Then she heard Maggie's voice in her head again. *Great.* Might as well get this over with now. She might still make it to The Bean on time. "Just give me the ticket." She dug in her purse and handed him her driver's license. The wind whistled as it whipped through the trees and she shivered under her parka.

. . .

RYAN COLTON STARED at Vera as she stood inches from him. She'd thrown the door open and got out as if she expected him to take a step back. He wasn't going anywhere.

Thin and leggy, Vera was tall for a woman, but still a few inches shorter than him. Her dark blue eyes and pale blonde hair drove men to distraction.

Unfortunately, he was no exception. "Now you want a ticket?" He took her license. Being this close to Vera addled his brain. He couldn't have heard right.

"Yeah, and I'd appreciate it if it's sometime this year." Vera put her hands on her hips.

He could smell the mint of her toothpaste. He was about to reconsider because everyone deserved one more chance and she looked so soft and beautiful this frigid morning. Now she insisted he cite her. Well, he wasn't about to disappoint her. He copied the information from her license, checked off her charge, put her speed in the blank provided, and signed the ticket. "Here you go." He tore off the sheet with no small amount of pleasure and held it out with her license. "You have a nice day."

Vera narrowed her eyes and ripped the paper out of his hand. "I'm going to try." She got back in her car and drove away slowly.

He got back in the cruiser and drove through town as the sun rose over the horizon and more cars began to populate the streets of Harte's Peak.

A year ago, he wouldn't have appreciated the graveyard shift like he did today. But only a few months ago he'd started to see everything in a new way. Now he saw the sunrise with a promise he'd never imagined before. Every morning felt like a new beginning, a chance to demonstrate his new self and to show God that he appreciated His grace.

Part of that meant covering the graveyard shift so that new family man, Jack, could spend the morning with his pregnant wife, Maggie.

Ryan was happy to take the shift. Even if it meant running into Vera the Speedster. If he were a revenue hound he'd know exactly where to find his meal ticket, but instead she'd managed to talk her way out of one the last three times she'd been pulled over.

Lonnie Smith, who still stammered like a schoolboy in her presence, had let her out of two tickets.

Yet he was in no position to judge since he'd also let Vera go with a verbal warning three weeks ago when she'd gazed into his eyes. He'd briefly remembered the old Ryan, the one who'd asked her out on a regular basis even though she had repeatedly turned him down.

Of all the townspeople who had heard about his conversion and baptism Vera seemed the least convinced. It would be an uphill battle to demonstrate to the people of Harte's Peak that he had changed. Vera, more than anyone else, reminded him of that fact.

Vera had finished up with the last of the morning rush customers when Annie Mc-Carthy, Maggie's replacement, arrived promptly at ten for her shift. Annie's nose ring and jet black hair made her look like a punk rocker. She was actually an unemployed school teacher. "Brrrr. Did you have any trouble getting in the door this morning? I had trouble getting out of my house." Annie tied on her apron.

"There were three customers waiting for me, and they helped me out."

"All kinds of gentlemen are out this morning. The heater in my car isn't working well, and when I thought my insides had congealed and turned into one solid block of ice, I saw Ryan Colton shoveling the entrance to Katie's bookstore. Just looking at him warmed me up."

"He's been a busy boy this morning." Vera smirked. Ryan had turned into a regular Boy Scout.

"I'm no fan of cops, but that man could change my mind," Annie sighed.

He might even change my mind. And if he'd ever ask her out again Vera might have to reconsider. He'd stopped asking several months ago, coincidentally, about the time he'd been baptized. Maybe he thought he was too good for her now.

"Since you're here, I'm going to the office and get some paperwork done." Vera took off her apron.

Six months ago, she'd taken a second mortgage on her home in order to make some improvements to the café, expanding to the storefront next door when it was vacated by the fabric shop that had closed its doors after twenty-five years in business. One of the additions included a private office in which she could adequately do personnel reviews and manage payroll.

Who could have known that shortly after the improvements were completed Harte's Peak tourism would take a swan dive?

Vera pulled out the file she had been avoiding and with shaking fingers dialed the number. She verified her information with the mortgage company's phone tree and waited for the representative to answer.

When she had the faceless person on the other end of the line, she tried to reason with them.

"Ms. Carrington, I see you're two months behind with your mortgage payment. I can take a payment right now over the phone for your convenience."

Vera winced. *For my convenience.* If she'd had the money to make the payment would she be making this embarrassing phone call? "I can't make a payment right now. But I have a few questions."

Apparently, a mortgagee asking questions threw the mortgage company for a loop. Vera was transferred to at least six different departments before she finally had the proper person on the line. She explained her position and waited for a response, barely able to breathe.

"The only way you were qualified for this loan was under our special interest-only program," this person droned on. "Of course, now that it's been a year your loan has adjusted, but you also need to start paying toward the principal. Your broker should have explained this to you." The representative's low pitched voice was more than a tad condescending.

Her broker had left town months ago when his business hit bottom. Now her payment had doubled. Vera thought she'd understood the fine print and terms of her refinance, but now she wished she'd hired a lawyer to translate it into plain English for her.

As she'd been taught to do, Vera listed all her assets in a column. At the top of that list sat the café. Sure, the economy had slowed, but the café would hold its own now that she'd trimmed expenses.

But even if there were buyers lining up for her café in this economy, she wasn't about to sell the one thing that had ever been truly hers.

No. She'd have to find another way to save her home.

RYAN HEADED home to catch a few hours of sleep after his shift before he headed over to the church's foundation meeting that afternoon. When their pastor had organized the *Home is Where the Heart Is* foundation in response to the record number of foreclosures in their county, Ryan saw it as a way to put his faith into action.

He often had to post the notices of foreclosure and orders to vacate on the homes and felt sick every time he did. In the small town, he was on a first name basis with some of the people who were about to lose their home. Sometimes it was too late to save the home, but the foundation was gifting first and last month's rent to displaced homeowners, and every now and then, they were able to provide enough money to get an owner caught up on their back payments. Lately, their meetings had been focused on raising money for the foundation. Unsettling ideas like a bachelor's auction had been proposed, and someone was trying to get in touch with a worship band to see if they'd play a free concert.

As he neared Vera's café, he pulled over. Maybe he'd drop in for a quick decaf and give her a chance to apologize. He'd only been doing his job this morning.

Annie was behind the counter, and Vera was nowhere in sight.

"Hey, Ryan. The usual?" Annie reached for the coffeepot.

"Decaf this time," he said.

He paid quickly and left the café nearly running into a man on his way inside.

"Sorry," he said and then did a double take.

"Kyle?"

"Hey, buddy." Kyle slapped him on the back.

Ryan hadn't seen Kyle Grant in years. Not since their days on the pro ski circuit. "What are you doing in Harte's Peak? You're not here for the tournament?"

"Yep, I am."

"Why would you do that? It's an open and you won't get much competition."

"Exactly. I could use the money and I like these opens from time to time. Keeps me

in shape for the bigger pro-circuit tournaments."

"Why come down so early? You won't
have to qualify, and it isn't 'til next month."

"Maybe I just wanted to drop in on an
old friend. You said if I ever landed in
Harte's Peak to look you up."

He had said that, but that was before
everything had changed. "Yeah."

"Anyway, the purse is only twenty-five
thousand this time around, but I came down
early to check out the competition. Although
I don't expect to have much."

"Twenty-five thousand?" Ryan allowed
himself to think of how far that could go toward shoring up the reserves of the foundation.

"Why? Are you thinking of entering?
That might actually make it fun for me."

"Nah. I'm out of shape. No match for
your skill anymore." With a little practice, he
might just be able take on his old friend, but
he hadn't been up on a pair of skis since the
accident that had sidelined his career.

"Tell the truth, bud. You never were."
Kyle elbowed him.

Ryan ignored that. "Where are you
staying?"

"I'm staying at the Lodge where I'll admit I do like the scenery. And I'm not just talking about these mountains." Kyle wiggled his eyebrows.

Right. Kyle referred to the women who flocked to these tournaments like groupies, treating the athletes like celebrities. He'd been on the end of that kind of attention in the past. "Good luck. If I can help, let me know. I'll be seeing you around."

"Wait a second. We should get together sometime. Tear up the town like we used to. The women of Harte's Peak won't know what hit them."

If anything, Ryan would have to keep his distance. He'd left that lifestyle behind and certainly wasn't going back to it now. "I'll leave you to that."

Kyle stared as if Ryan had just said that skiing was a sport for sissies.

Ryan would need to take some time and explain to Kyle that he'd changed. Even if he wasn't quite sure where to begin.

Chapter 2

Vera didn't see that she had any other choice. She'd have to visit her mother and beg for help. If she could get current with her mortgage, she could relax and breathe. Even better, a major ski tournament would take place in one month, and the publicity would boost tourism.

At a Chamber of Commerce meeting, she'd heard every lodge in town was booked solid for the event. All of those tourists would be looking for a warm cup of coffee both before and after the slopes.

Vera locked up her office and made her way to the uncrowded café. "I have to take a drive to Sonoma."

"That's a two hour drive. Will you be

back later, or do you want me to close?" Annie asked.

"Do you mind?" She'd never had Annie close shop alone before, but the time had come.

Annie grinned ear to ear, obviously feeling she'd earned a measure of trust.

The drive down the mountain and into the valley was a little like leaving one world and entering another. In the mountains, pine trees that were filled with dollops of snow bowing the branches became green pine trees, their branches empty except for the occasional squirrel.

Soon enough she arrived in the valley, where even the rain could not change its pristine appearance. The streets might have been paved with gold for all the money here. Ava Carrington lived in the same old and established neighborhood where Vera and her older sister, Amy, had grown up.

Vera had called ahead and heard the measure of surprise in her mother's voice. They hadn't spoken since the holidays, and those conversations had been strained. Pulling into the long circular driveway Vera held her breath.

Maybe this wasn't such a good idea.

But Mom had more money than she could ever possibly spend. She was a frugal woman, a fact she never hesitated to bring up around Vera.

"Hi, Mom." Vera hugged her mother in the entryway.

"Let's have some tea. I waited for you." Mom led her into the elegant dining room.

Vera glanced at the grandfather clock in the entryway. She'd arrived a few minutes after noon, and her mother, who fancied herself English, served tea at high noon. Though Mom never fully comprehended that high tea in the UK was served later in the day, the ritual used to comfort Vera. No matter what else happened in the world, she knew at noon they'd be having tea.

Even on the day that Dad had left them once and for all, Mom had called her girls into the dining room where both Vera and Amy had sipped tea through their tears.

"You look too thin," Mom said through pursed lips.

A new record. She'd been in her mother's house less than ten minutes this time. "I've gained ten pounds in the past year."

"Well, it doesn't look like it. You know how this makes your sister feel. She can't help it if she's meaty like me." Mom dropped four cubes of sugar in Vera's teacup without asking.

"Mom, you're hardly meaty."

"You're naturally thin like your father." Her mother winced as though the tea tasted bitter, but Vera knew the bitterness came from the memory her mother's words had churned up. "I'm only asking you to think of how that makes Amy feel."

"Amy and I are fine. We talk every other day." As usual, the problem was in Mom's mind. A mind like a steel trap that couldn't let go of the past.

Vera had made a mistake coming here. Mom pushed the cookies in Vera's direction.

Vera wasn't hungry, but she took an angry bite out of one.

"So why are you here?" Mom's brown eyes narrowed.

"Can't I just come by to visit?"

"You can, but you don't." Her mother sighed.

"How's the man who escorted you to Christmas dinner? I can't remember his name. Eddie?"

Leave it to her mom to remember the exact name of the man she'd brought home for the holiday, someone she had not seen or heard from since that day.

Vera chose not to answer. Instead, she shoved another cookie in her mouth.

"Is he the latest casualty in your string of men?" Mom continued.

"I haven't seen him, and we weren't serious anyway." She didn't need any man in her life, but no need to bother trying to convince her mother of that fact.

"I'm not surprised. You'll probably never settle down. You don't want to meet the right man, do you? You're just like your father."

Mom's acid tongue burned into Vera's heart. Mom never meant comparisons to her father as a compliment.

"I did settle down once. Don't you remember?" Mom never saw past Vera's ex-husband's money to see his faults.

"He was a good man." Mom poured more tea.

A good man? Vera winced, her fists tightening. She took a deep breath and let it out. "I know how much you liked him."

"He took care of you, didn't he? You don't know how lucky you are."

"Lucky?"

"Don't pretend you don't realize how beautiful you are. You could get a man anytime you want one. If only you would decide on one and stick with him. How hard is that?"

"I did pick a man." Vera held the fragile looking teacup so tightly she feared it might burst into a hundred little pieces.

"Yes, you did do that. Several, in fact. Now if you could learn to hang on to one."

Like you hung on to my father? There was no point to this. She couldn't ask her mother for help. She'd tell her to find another husband. She placed the empty cup on the table and stood. "I need to go."

"What did I say?" Mom's eyes widened.

"Nothing."

Her mother pushed away from the table. "Go ahead. Leave. You do that well. You shouldn't be so sensitive when I'm trying to give you a little advice."

Vera bit her lip for a long moment, staring at her mother. Then she shook her head. "I can get advice from my friends. From Amy. When it comes to my mother, sometimes all I want is a hug."

And that wasn't going to happen. Mom touched only when necessary: to straighten a flyaway hair, brush bangs out of eyes, flick away a piece of lint. The last time she'd embraced Vera had been on her wedding day.

"I'll call you later." Vera's eyes brimmed with tears as she walked out. She'd have to find another way to get out of her financial mess.

Chapter 3

The next day, after the aspiring screenwriters and novelists powered down and shut their laptops, Vera shooed the last of her customers out the door and closed up shop. No matter how exhausting, work was her one saving grace—something she loved. Who would have thought that a former fashion model could be happy making coffee and sweeping floors?

Because this was hers. She'd built this business, it was hers, and no one could take it away.

Not without a fight.

Her friend Maggie had dropped off a brochure last week. Sure, they helped home and business owners stave off foreclosure, but the foundation was associated with the church. She'd have to find another savior. There was still one more person she could call, yet Vera's stomach twisted when she thought of him.

She climbed into the expensive sedan she would probably not drive much longer and drove the short distance home. Another storm front was expected to come in tomorrow, and the gray and stormy skies reflected her mood.

Vera's opened the door to her home, wondering how many more times she might have that privilege.

Her Beagle-mix rescue, Stin, met Vera at the door, jumping and spinning in circles. The only thing missing was the pink tutu, and then Stin could join the circus.

No matter how long Vera would be gone, Stin greeted her as though she'd been missing for years.

Vera picked her up and nuzzled her. "Hello, girl. I'm happy to see you, too."

She put Stin down and looked through her mail. A letter from the mortgage lender caused her breath to hitch.

She tore open the envelope and read the official looking notice. The letter stated *Notice of Default* in bold letters. *Dear Homeowner: Your loan is in default, and you must make immediate payment or face legal action.*

She skimmed over the paperwork before her mind shut itself off.

Stin wagged her tail, jumped up, and licked Vera's hand as though she sensed her distress.

"I'm sorry, Stin. You can't cheer me up today."

The bank would be closed already. Anyway, she had no idea what she could say. She didn't have the money to come up with this month's payment, much less bring her mortgage current.

This home was too large for her, a fact she had realized only after purchasing and making numerous upgrades. She'd paid too much for the granite countertops, cherry wood cabinets, and kitchen island. It was beautifully and tastefully decorated, courtesy of her sister, Amy, who definitely had talent. She loved her home, but she certainly didn't need four bedrooms or matching his-and-her sinks.

Vera rummaged through her roll-top desk for the list she'd made the night before. She'd thought of every person she could ask for money and crossed off the majority of them within minutes.

She couldn't ask her sister. Amy and her new husband had married last year and joined their blended family. Amy clipped coupons and went to the spa only when Vera paid. If Amy had any inkling how much money Vera had spent in the past few years, their relationship might not be as harmonious as it continued to be.

Still, there was one name that remained on the list. One she'd written down and crossed off a half-dozen times. They hadn't spoken in years, and she'd hoped to keep it that way.

"Don't look at me like that, Stin. I'm desperate."

Even Stin realized it was a bad idea as she cocked her head to the side. Sometimes, Vera swore the dog could read her mind.

She stared at the name on her list. Kevin. Vera had to look in her old address book for his phone number. She'd long ago removed all traces of it from her cell. The bank letter convinced her of the seriousness of her situation, and she punched in the number.

"Hello? Hello? Who is this?" Kevin sounded as brusque as she remembered him.

Vera hung up before she could change her mind or listen to another word out of his mouth. The money Kevin loaned would come with strings of venom attached to it. She might never free herself again. No. She couldn't have him back in her life no matter how bad things were. "You were right, Stin. Are you happy now?"

Stin wagged her tail.

Vera put her face in her hands. "Don't worry. I'll figure something out."

"You're a little later than I expected," Annie said from behind the counter.

"I had some errands to run." After a couple of weeks of advertising, Vera had met with a prospective buyer for her car. One less payment to make would help ease her burden, and the vehicle was still in prime condition and only three years old. The man said he'd call her back after running the numbers. If he accepted her price and terms, she'd have enough money left over to buy a used car.

She tied on her apron and stuck her hair in a ponytail. Thankfully, business had already picked up and hope seemed to lie just beyond the horizon. Some of the competitive skiers had arrived early.

One of them had become annoying already, flirting with her daily. He'd introduced himself as Kyle, and he claimed he was going to win the title. Narcissism dripped from his pores like sweat, but Vera smiled and encouraged him. She couldn't afford to alienate anyone now.

Vera and Annie made a great team as they worked in synchronization, Vera taking the orders at the register and Annie filling them. The warm and rich scent of coffee, the hiss and steam of the espresso machine, reminded Vera that people still drank coffee in tough times. For that, she was grateful.

The door opened.

"Good morning, Katie," she called out to one of her regulars, the owner of the small bookstore two doors down.

She took the order for another one of her regulars, handed it to Annie to fill, then headed back to the register to get the next order.

Her next customer stood in front of her and she almost didn't recognize him at first.

His hair was no longer only gray at the temples. The wrinkles on his face were a little craggier. He was impeccably dressed in what appeared to be a silk suit and staggeringly out of place in Harte's Peak.

"Kevin," she managed. Why had he traveled from New Mexico?

"Vera. Beautiful, as always."

"What are you doing here?" she snapped.

"Visiting. Aren't you going to ask for my order?" Vera blinked. "Of course."

Perhaps the best way to deal with him would be to pretend that it wasn't at all unusual to see him for the first time in eight years, right after she'd made an ill- advised phone call. Apparently, like a shark, he'd smelled blood.

She ignored him through the morning rush, watching him out of the corner of her eye.

He sat at a table nearby, a copy of the San Francisco Chronicle in his hands.

"Annie, I'm going to take a short break." Vera took off her apron and moved to sit down across the table from her ex-husband. Sooner or later, she was going to have to deal with the elephant in the room.

He looked up from the paper, a smug

smile on his face. He obviously enjoyed her curiosity.

"Kevin, let's not play games. You and I both know you're here for a reason."

He put down his paper. "You're a business owner now?"

"That's right. I own this café." She crossed her arms. "I answered your question. Now you answer mine."

"Fine. How much do you need?" Pleasure lilted from his baritone voice. He wanted an opportunity to throw his money around, to feel important. And he obviously thought she was about to give him one.

"You think I need money?" One lousy phone call in a moment of weakness and he'd tracked her down like a bloodhound.

"Why else would you call?"

A memory flashed in her mind of his last words to her. *Someday, you'll need something from me. You'll call and I can't wait for that day.*

"Let's get this straight. I didn't call you. I dialed your number. And hung up. It doesn't count."

Knowing that he'd looked her up and tracked her down felt like a violation. Her address wasn't a state secret, but they weren't pen pals, either. She'd wanted a clean break, and he hadn't had a choice in the matter.

Kevin folded his paper perfectly in half, pressing the ends down like it was an origami project. "I forgot how smart you are. It was much easier when you played dumb. Anyway, it only took me a few phone calls to find out that you're hopelessly over extended. You're about to lose your house."

Under the table, Vera clenched her hands into fists. "And how is that any business of yours? You didn't hear me ask for money, did you?"

"No, I realize you're still too proud to do that, so I thought I'd save you the trouble." His voice rose above the din of the café.

She couldn't get into a war of words with Kevin now. If she challenged him too much, he'd make a scene. If she didn't challenge him enough, he wouldn't get the message. "Lower your voice. If I'm over extended, it's only a temporary thing. I can take care of myself."

"I don't doubt that's what you think. But the truth is, you've got a nice little operation going here. I checked that out, too. This café has great potential, like this little town does. Once we drag it into this century."

Finally, the real reason he'd come. "This café is not for sale."

Kevin curled his lips. "We'll see about that."

"No, we won't."

"There it is. Your least attractive quality. Stupid, stubborn pride. If it wasn't for you, I'd have children. But you were such a lousy wife you couldn't even get that most basic function right." Kevin's voice was loud enough that several of the patrons turned their heads in his direction.

Still, she hoped they hadn't heard his stinging words.

No matter how many times he said those words, they never stopped having the power to take her breath away. She stood and gathered every ounce of her courage. "I'd like you to leave. Now."

"Is there a problem?" Ryan approached, coffee mug in hand.

Vera narrowed her eyes at Kevin and then glanced in Ryan's direction. Ryan was on duty, armed, tall, strong, and able. For once, he was right where she wanted him to be and not right behind her with his flashing lights.

"No, officer. I'm leaving." Kevin stood and smiled as he walked toward the doors.

Ryan looked at Vera, his eyebrows knotted together. "Who was that guy?"

"You don't want to know."

THE GUY'S hair was Wall Street gray, and he looked like he bled money. Ryan didn't know much about fashion, but he wouldn't be surprised if the suit the man wore cost a grand.

But what concerned him the most was the look in Vera's eyes. He's seen that same apprehension on the faces of victims. Something was definitely going on.

Ryan stepped closer to Vera. "You didn't answer my question. Is there a problem?" The way the guy had looked at Vera was a problem for Ryan. He wanted to wipe that leer right off his face.

"Not anymore." Vera smiled, but the look was forced, and the smile didn't reach her eyes. In fact, her blue eyes were a little swollen almost like she'd been crying.

"You doing all right?"

She looked smaller and even thinner than normal.

"I'm fine." Vera turned away. "Back to work for me."

"I see you have a crowd here most mornings." Hopefully, she was happy about that. He'd made sure to tell Kyle about the best coffee in town and encouraged him to tell his fellow competitors.

"And afternoons," Annie said from behind the counter.

"Get them coming and going?" Ryan approached the counter. "Have you met my friend Kyle yet?"

"Kyle is a friend of yours?" Vera asked. "I guess I shouldn't be too surprised."

"What's that supposed to mean?" As if he didn't know. Kyle was a flirt who loved women and usually had two or more with him. Vera probably still thought of Ryan in the same way even though he hadn't flirted with her in months.

"Nothing. Kyle's a good guy. Always tells us how he's going to win first place. Not shy at all." Vera laughed.

"He's always got a joke for me," Annie said.

"Yeah, well, twenty-five thousand dollars is his primary motivation for being here." Ryan shrugged.

"What do you mean?" Vera leaned in across the service counter.

"Twenty-five thousand dollars. It's the purse offered for first place in the skiing tournament next month. Granted, it's a drop in the bucket for him."

Vera folded her arms across her chest. "That much money for skiing? Who are you trying to kid?"

"These tournaments draw competitive skiers from all over. Kyle lives in Colorado."

"I can't believe they'll give someone that much money to ski," Vera said.

He didn't like the look in her eyes. Not at all. "Not to ski. To win. It's an open, but you still have to qualify to enter."

"This is interesting. As it happens, I love to ski. I always have." Vera wrapped her arms around her small waist.

"Vera, you don't mean it," Annie said.

"No. Don't even think about it," Ryan added.

"Both of you mind your own business. Now Ryan, tell me all about this contest."

He had no idea why she would want to enter the tournament. And she had no clue what kind of competition she'd be up against.

"It might be too late to enter," he stalled. "Any amateur that isn't already ranked will have to qualify with their time before the tournament."

"Either you tell me, or I'll ask Kyle when he comes in. I'm sure he'd be more than happy to talk about it. Might give him a chance to talk about himself, too."

Ryan sighed. "Fine. I'll tell you everything you want to know."

Vera came from behind the counter and sat down at an empty table as she waved for Ryan to join her.

"How can I enter?"

"Whoa, let's talk about this. When's the last time you skied?"

"What does that matter?"

"You can't be serious. Do you even remember the last time?"

"I grew up skiing. My dad took us every year."

"That's nice, but family vacations don't make you a skier. Did you know I ran the pro ski circuit before I became a deputy?"

"Did you?"

"Maybe I could enter and try to place. It's been a long time and even I'd have to qualify again. It's a long shot for me, too, but

I have a better chance. If I win, and that's a big 'if,' I'll give you the money." Even as he said the words, his body tensed. He hadn't been on the slopes since the accident.

Twenty-five thousand dollars was a lot of money and she obviously needed it, although he wasn't sure why. Still, she had to be desperate to consider this and too proud to admit she needed the money. And even though the thought of getting back up on skis caused him to break out in a sweat, he'd do it for her. It would all come back to him.

She seemed to consider it for a nanosecond and then shook her head. "No. I don't need your charity. I can ski the slopes myself."

"Be reasonable. Even if you make a qualifying time, you'll be up against someone like Kyle who does this for a living." Why was she so stubborn? And why on earth did she need that much money?

"That's fine, I don't scare easily."

"You don't have to tell me that." He sighed. "Do you have all your equipment?"

"I have it all somewhere at my house."

Great. Any skier who couldn't locate their equipment at a moment's notice wouldn't be ready for a tournament like this.

"I'll check out your equipment and make sure everything's in working order. I'll help you with that unless you consider it charity. I wouldn't want to offend you."

"Actually, I probably need a coach. Maybe some refresher lessons." She nodded.

At last, some logic from her. "We can go the slopes day after tomorrow. I'm not working, and I can see if there is anything in particular you need to work on."

"Thanks. I do appreciate this." She smiled. His pulse quickened. "It's no big deal."

"One more thing. What does it cost to enter?"

He leveled a stare at her. "Five hundred dollars."

"Five—hundred?" Vera bit her lower lip.

"I can lend it to you."

Vera was obviously in some kind of financial bind. He didn't think she'd resort to this, no matter how competitive her nature.

"What makes you think I need you to lend it to me? I've got it." She turned and went back behind the counter.

But she wasn't fooling him.

While he trained her, he'd get to the

bottom of the real problem one way or another.

SNOW.

Three feet of fresh snow was expected by day's end, and Ryan imagined the usual traffic complications that went along with it. The skiers, including Kyle, who spent their days on the ski slopes in preparation for the tournament, would welcome it. Ryan had heard plenty of complaints about the hard-packed snow giving way to more injuries than normal. He threw a pair of chains in his truck and drove to Vera's home to assess her ski equipment. Although he'd at times envied people who lived in her sterling neighborhood, the past year had taught him that appearances were often deceiving. The homes had lost more than half their value and for anyone who was forced to leave the area it meant the loss of a small fortune.

He'd been praying that she would see the error of entering this type of tournament, but he knew he wouldn't be able to talk Vera out of her harebrained idea. Best to be nearby to help when she fell in the cold, wet snow or broke a nail and reconsidered.

As he pulled up to her home, Vera stood in the open garage sorting through boxes. An older foreign sedan looked out of place in the driveway, and Vera's fancy car was nowhere in sight.

"Let me help you with that." He grabbed a box just out of her reach and handed it to her.

"I think my boots might be in here." She opened the box and began rummaging through it.

"Whose car is that?" Ryan pointed to the vehicle.

"Mine."

"What happened to your other car?" He regretted his words as the truth hit him. She'd downsized. A smart thing to do if she had money trouble, but it must have been difficult.

"Maybe I'm tired of you chasing me down and giving me speeding tickets. I figured if I got a slower car, I'd be better off." She shrugged as though it were no big deal and his heart clenched. Everyone in town knew how much Vera loved that car.

"Smart move."

He helped her to locate and stack her outdated equipment. She couldn't compete with what she had. Still, they'd be worth trying out on the slopes. He didn't want her to stress about spending any money. If nothing else, his old equipment would be better than what she owned.

"Are you sure I can't talk you out of this?" He grew increasingly worried about Vera on the slopes with amateurs who were one race away from qualifying on the pro circuit. She wasn't anywhere in their league. And worse, she could get seriously injured.

"You ought to know better than that by now. Besides, isn't it usually me doing the talking? Out of speeding tickets and such?"

"You are pretty good at that. I guess I could use some lessons from you in that department."

"Sure. After you help me with this ski tournament."

"You've got a deal."

Now, if he could only convince her to let him know what was going on instead of her risking life and limb for the purse. *Lord, I'm going to need Your help here.*

Chapter 4

Only expert skiers were aware that one of the top- rated resorts in the country stood outside Harte's Peak. Dodge Ridge Ski Lodge was one of the best kept secret of the Sierras, with its expert trails and a fully implemented ski school. A little something for everyone.

And one of the reasons Ryan had landed here several years ago. When he'd abandoned the competitive ski tour, the desire to be in the mountains had never quite left. Of course, flying down them at high rates of speed was another story. But these hills— the trails—represented a past from which he couldn't hide.

Ryan scoped out the skiers dotting the

hills wearing black, white, and the range of rainbow colored parkas. Clearly, Kyle was not the only one who had arrived early. By the looks of the money spent on equipment alone, Vera should be worried. And now he was apprehensive, too.

And not only about Vera. Uncomfortable memories of the last time he'd skied pricked his mind, but after all this time there should be no reason he couldn't get back up on a pair. At one time, the sport had been second only to breathing. He shook off the worry that anyone could take away the peace he'd found. Not Kyle, and certainly not sliding down these mountains.

Vera waited for him outside the check-in, all suited up with her competitor lift ticket displayed on her pink and black jacket. "You showed up."

"What did you expect?" The thought that she'd entertained the notion that he might not even show up for their first training lesson stung.

"I don't know. I thought maybe it was a line." She bit her lip.

"That's not me." He stared at her. "Not anymore."

"All right, I apologize." She shrugged.

Sure, there was a time when he would have done or said anything to spend time with a pretty woman. Those days were gone. Sooner or later, everyone would get the message, even Vera. He reminded himself to be patient.

He was here to show Vera part of that change and even though her blue eyes reminded him of the San Francisco Bay, it would have no effect on his ability to teach her. This would be a strictly teacher-student relationship.

"So did you sign up yet?" Ryan glanced in the direction of the contest headquarters. A sign announced that the deadline to enter was in two days.

"I'm about to do that now. I called ahead and they agreed to waive my entrance fee."

"How'd you do that?"

"Business. I'm a member of the Chamber and I agreed to serve as secretary for the next year. It's the hardest position to fill."

Ryan nodded. Vera apparently had a real knack for negotiating.

Chip, a local teenager, stood behind the counter for sign-ups and recognized Ryan right away. "You entering?"

"Not me." He turned to Vera.

"Huh. Hello," Chip said, gawking. The kid was eighteen and one of the many who seemed to lose the power of speech around Vera. "Uh, here." Chip reached for a clipboard, but it fell out of his hands. He bent down to pick it up off the floor and gazed at Vera with a lopsided grin. "Sorry."

Vera reached for the clipboard and filled out the paper work. "This sure is a lot of information you need. Do I also have to give you a blood sample?"

"Oh, no, you don't." Chip put up his hands.

"She's kidding," Ryan said. "I think."

"Of course I am." Vera laughed. "I'll need dinner before I give any blood."

Chip laughed loudly. "I never knew you were funny."

Containing the eye roll, Ryan steered Vera toward the ski lifts.

With his own lift ticket pinned, Ryan suggested the bunny hill. It would be far away from the competitors and they'd have some privacy for some refresher lessons.

"No way. Are you purposely trying to embarrass me? I haven't been on the bunny hill since I was ten."

"Let's be reasonable. We'd be out of their way while we go over a few things."

"I don't want to be out of their way."

"You might rethink that. Have you taken a look at your competition?" He glanced pointedly in that direction.

"But you haven't seen what I can do yet." Vera's blue eyes pierced into him.

"Have it your way. Let's start with the moderate hill. I'll ride along with you and check out your form."

In the next moment he hoped she realized he meant her agility and not her long and shapely legs. He'd barely noticed those. *C'mon, Ryan, stop second guessing your every word.*

The first few minutes and he was already annoyed with her. The word *stubborn* came to mind. His nerves pricked like a sharp blade and bickering with Vera would help nothing.

They headed toward the ski lift.

Kyle was there with a large group. Some would have called it an entourage. Kyle never seemed to be alone.

"Hey, Ryan, what are you doing here? Did you change your mind?" Kyle yelled from the front of the line.

"He's helping me," Vera answered.

"Helping you do what?" Kyle raised his eyebrows.

"She's entering the tournament." Ryan wished he could wipe that smirk off Kyle's face. That Kyle would be highly favored to win didn't change the fact that he could use a speck of humility, apparently still a foreign concept to the man.

"How long have you skied?" Kyle asked.

"About twenty years, give or take," she snapped.

"Huh, well you ought to be pretty good, then." Kyle grinned.

"I am." Vera smiled.

Kyle eyed Vera like a wolf would a lone rabbit.

After some instruction and reminders to control speed with the wedge, Vera was ready for a first run.

"All right, show me what you got. I'll be right behind you."

Vera started, and he pushed off after her.

His knees buckled almost immediately, and his vision blurred. Maybe this hadn't been such a great idea. He let out a breath and struggled for focus. *Get back on the edge.* That precipice he'd thrived on was now accompanied with much more than a quickened heart beat and a surge of adrenaline. This time his heart pounded, and he broke out in a sweat even as the cold wind whipped across his face.

He could do this.

He didn't want to be the kind of man he used to be when he'd ridden the competitive trails. That man hadn't known the Lord, and he sure hadn't cared much about people. Only winning.

He slowed down to observe Vera critically since this wasn't his race. That reminder steadied him, and he got his legs back. While her ski skills were not at the beginner level, in comparison to the others flying down the hill and catching air, he still had reason for concern.

Vera, a vision in pink and black against the white snowy back drop, whipped down the hill. She was fast all right, in a way that worried the heck out of him but didn't surprise him in the slightest. Vera the Speedster. The control, or lack of it, was another matter. She wobbled on her skis and at times looked like she'd face plant at any minute. The loss of control at those speeds could be disastrous. He considered that he might still be able to talk her out of this idea if he could only find the right words.

They met at the bottom of the slope. "That was pretty good, but—"

"But what?" Vera frowned.

"There's always room for improvement."

"Why, officer, what did you have in mind?" Her tone was light, teasing.

"You're fast all right, but you need better control." She needed to take this seriously.

"Better control? You don't think I can handle myself?" Her voice rose in protest.

"Are you here to learn or argue with me?" The girl had no fear, and he considered offering her some of his own. Accidents did happen on the slopes, and she'd do well to remember it.

She shrugged. "Fine. Show me."

Ryan tried to find an example in the skiers on the slope. He pointed out Kyle, as his old friend flew past the expert slope at what appeared to be near the speed of light. Kyle was her real competition. Getting her to see past her rose-colored glasses would be another matter altogether. *Tread lightly, Ryan.*

"See how he crouches down a bit as he rounds that trail?"

"Right. I'll try that." She bent her knees.

He grabbed her gloved hand before she pushed off. "Wait a minute. I'm not done."

"There's more?"

"I notice you started off with the French fry position. And you're going to gain speed that way, but try the wedge next time for better control as you start out."

Vera's eyebrows rose. "The French fry? The wedge?"

So she didn't know ski lingo. He translated and explained how the wedge controlled speed while the French fry meant immediate speed.

They took the ski lift up several more times that afternoon, and each time, Vera gained a little more control. By the end of the day, she appeared exhausted and dragged behind him. For once, she kept quiet.

The days when he could ski for hours without being winded were a part of his past now, but so was the constant state of panic he'd lived in both on and off the slopes. All things considered, he'd made a better trade.

Vera took off her helmet and shook her wet hair out. She ran a hand along the helmet hair plastered to her crimson red cheeks. "Do I really have to wear this every time?"

"Don't even think about taking it off when you're on the slopes," Ryan said.

"Yes, sir." She saluted. Her beaming smile, like the sun breaking through on a cloudy day, unsettled him.

They followed some of the skiers into the lodge for their first real break of the day.

Kyle was there holding court.

A brief chill rolled through Ryan as he recalled doing much the same in the old days. Before everything had spiraled out of control.

He offered to get Vera a hot chocolate and by the time he returned, Kyle had joined Vera at their table. Kyle leaned in to Vera as though telling her a secret. In the next second, Vera threw her head back and laughed. Ryan tensed, reminded of why he'd never let a girl he cared about be alone with Kyle.

"Hey." Ryan set Vera's mug in front of her.

"Hey, Champ." Kyle leaned back, arms crossed. "I was telling Vera that you should be the one on the slopes. You can cut the trails with the best of us."

"That was a long time ago." A time he'd rather forget.

"Until his injury, he was my biggest threat." Kyle kept talking, and Ryan found himself wishing he had a mute button. The last thing he wanted Vera to hear about was the person he used to be—the one who would do anything to win.

"What injury?" Vera cocked her head to the side.

She looked genuinely interested.

"It was nothing." They were edging near dangerous territory for him. Parts of his past life he'd rather leave buried where they belonged.

"He hasn't told you?" Kyle pressed.

"I don't talk about it." Ryan glared at Kyle.

Kyle took the cue and rose from the table. "Excuse me, doll. I have some friends waiting for me."

"Wow. That guy is a real piece of work." Vera rolled her eyes. "I can't believe anyone could tolerate him for longer than a minute or two."

Ryan relaxed immediately.

Vera hadn't been taken in by Kyle.

"He believes his own good press. Happens to the best of them."

"I guess. It didn't happen to you, did it?"

"Where did you think I got the idea that you'd go out with me?" In the competitive ski days he had as many dates as he could handle. He'd carried that same attitude over when he'd become a police officer.

"You were rather cocky when you came into town. So that's where that comes from?"

"Maybe." Winning tournaments meant money, prestige, and attention. And something that felt like love, which he now recognized as counterfeit.

Vera leaned back in her chair and studied him. "I can't figure you out, Colton."

"I think you tried once."

"Are you saying I was wrong?"

"Not then. But you are now. Listen, I appreciate that you only tried to talk me out of the contest once today," Vera said.

Ryan walked with her to her car. She popped open the trunk to take off her boots, and he did the same.

"The day's not over yet," he said. "But I must admit you're a decent skier."

Vera beamed. "I tried to tell you. I owe

you a nice home-cooked meal if you're not busy."

"You can cook?" The idea struck him as funny, and he put his hand to his chest in mock shock.

"Of course. I considered opening my own restaurant once. Before I bought the cafe."

"You should know one other thing about me: I'll never turn down a free meal. Remember, I'm a public servant."

He followed her car back into town as the freshly fallen snow created a line of cars stopped in the other direction along Route 129. Ryan spotted one of their deputies out on the highway assisting stranded motorists. Good thing he'd brought a second set of chains and insisted that Vera put them on her vehicle.

Tonight, he'd find out exactly why she had this death wish. The competition he'd seen on the slopes today made Vera's chances at winning a long shot. He didn't want to crush her spirit, but he had to make her see the truth somehow.

She needed money, evidenced by the sale of the car, which hadn't fooled him. It had nothing to do with speeding tickets. If he could get to the bottom of the problem, maybe he could help in a real way. But first Vera would have to trust him.

And he was curious about the Wall Street guy, because there was something going on there, even though it was none of his business.

A small tri-color Beagle greeted them at the entrance to Vera's home.

"This is Stin." Vera bent down to pet its head.

Stin took one look at him and, tail between her legs, ran out of the room headed toward the back of the house.

"Was it something I said?" Growing up, he'd had three dogs and friend's pets usually sensed the animal lover in him.

"Don't take it personally. Stin doesn't like men." Vera shrugged. "I think it has to do with the deep voice."

He stepped into the house and what seemed a simulated photograph inside an issue of *Better Homes and Gardens.* Not that he read that magazine, but his mother used to get a copy every month. She'd drool over places that looked like Vera's home.

Apparently owning a café could be a lu-crative business, which made him even more confused. Hardwood floors ran the length of the hallway to the kitchen, which was obviously the focal point of the home with its black granite countertops and cherry wood cabinets. A large kitchen island sat in the center. The hanging pots from a hook above the island were owned by someone who took pride in having the best tools for the job. Finally, some common ground.

"Have a seat." She waved toward the couch.

He didn't feel dressed well enough to sit on the couch, so he pulled out a kitchen stool by the counter.

Vera pulled out a knife from the butcher block and reached for the cutting board inches from him.

"Can I help?" Surely, she wouldn't want him to because there was something going on there, even though it was none of his business.

A small tri-color Beagle greeted them at the entrance to Vera's home.

"This is Stin." Vera bent down to pet its head.

Stin took one look at him and, tail between her legs, ran out of the room headed toward the back of the house.

"Was it something I said?" Growing up, he'd had three dogs and friend's pets usually sensed the animal lover in him.

"Don't take it personally. Stin doesn't like men." Vera shrugged. "I think it has to do with the deep voice."

He stepped into the house and what seemed a simulated photograph inside an issue of *Better Homes and Gardens.* Not that he read that magazine, but his mother used to get a copy every month. She'd drool over places that looked like Vera's home.

Apparently owning a café could be a lucrative business, which made him even more confused. Hardwood floors ran the length of the hallway to the kitchen, which was obviously the focal point of the home with its black granite countertops and cherry wood cabinets. A large kitchen island sat in the center. The hanging pots from a hook above the island were owned by someone who took pride in having the best tools for the job. Finally, some common ground.

"Have a seat." She waved toward the couch.

He didn't feel dressed well enough to sit on the couch, so he pulled out a kitchen stool by the counter.

Vera pulled out a knife from the butcher block and reached for the cutting board inches from him.

"Can I help?" Surely, she wouldn't want him to sit. He got up to assist and bumped right into Vera's shoulder.

As she turned to face him, they stood short inches from each other.

He breathed in the scent of her honeysuckle shampoo.

"You do not want to mess with a woman and her knife." She smirked.

"I'm not crazy if that's what you mean." He grinned.

"Ryan, I know you want to help. Right now, you can help by sitting down." She pointed to the stool.

Chastised, he sat and observed as she chopped vegetables with expert skill. She was right about the fact that he wouldn't want to get between her and that knife.

She flitted about the kitchen, filling a pot with water and throwing the vegetables in a pan. They sizzled, and the smell of garlic filled the air.

"Smells great." Whatever she was cooking made his stomach growl.

"Pasta primavera. We need our carbs after a workout like the one we had today."

When she smiled every angle of her face relaxed, and Ryan had to remind himself that he'd sworn off women until he met the one he would marry. As it turned out, he hadn't dated in months, but who was counting?

Still, he couldn't stop appreciating Vera any more than he could turn away from a red sunset.

"I haven't seen Jack for a while, but I saw Maggie last week, and she's huge." Vera stirred the pot of pasta.

"Jack is settling in to his newly elected position. I can't complain. Pretty nice when your best friend is also your boss."

"I hope Maggie would say the same thing."

"Something tells me she would." Kind of strange that their best friends were married to each other.

He had a lot to be grateful for, and one of those things was his friendship with Jack and Maggie Butler. When Jack started going to church with Maggie and her daughter Lexi, he invited Ryan along. After several invites, Ryan had gone, and because of Jack's diligence, he'd found his freedom and the identity he now had in Christ.

Most of the town of Harte's Peak had come out for his baptism six months ago. Vera hadn't shown up, but she didn't attend church. Also notably absent was his father, who lived out of state and thought Ryan had joined some type of cult. He still had a lot of work to do on that end. Right now, his work involved one stubborn blonde and a contest. Enough of the pleasantries.

"The thought still occurs to me that I might have an easier time qualifying for this race." He played with the silverware Vera had placed on the counter.

"You can banish that thought right out of your head." She waved the knife in his direction.

"It's not going anywhere." He stared.

"Keep it to yourself then. It was fun today. I haven't had so much fun since my dad took me." A distant look appeared in her eyes.

"Your dad liked to ski?"

They had that in common as well. Ryan's dad had introduced him to the sport, pushed him into the competitions and the touring lifestyle. Ted Colton had enjoyed the lifestyle, too— enjoyed it right up to the steps of the courthouse where the divorce hearing had been held. Ryan's mother still blamed the ski tournament tours for destroying her family, and for the first time in his life, Ryan realized she'd been right all along.

"Yeah, he used to take my sister and me skiing every season. Then he got himself a new family." Vera set two plates on the counter.

"Sorry." Ryan's jaw tightened.

They had more in common than either of them realized.

"Don't be. I can't say that I blame my dad entirely. You would have to know my mother to understand. Although, if I think about it, I'm not sure what came first. The divorce or my mother's bitterness. I guess they're both intertwined."

"Did your mother remarry as well?"

"Are you kidding? Not when she can be a living martyr."

"My mother never remarried either. Instead she clung to my brother and me like we were a lifeline. I was the first to leave home, but my younger brother followed shortly after and joined the Army. Anything to get away from home."

This conversation was good. Maybe if he confided in her, eventually she'd let her guard down enough to tell him why winning this contest seemed so important to her.

"At least she paid attention to you." Vera placed a pitcher of water in front of him.

"If by attention you mean smothering, then, yes."

Vera laughed and the sparkle in her eyes caused his knees to nearly buckle for the second time in one day.

VERA SERVED dinner at the counter, and they ate on the kitchen stools. No need to get fancy with Ryan. This wasn't a date, and she wanted to make that clear. Men like Ryan, church-going men, were to be her friends and nothing more. Even if those brown eyes, that devastating smile, and his athletic form reminded her that once she'd thought him a very attractive man. A little too handsome maybe. She'd quickly placed him in the compete-with mirror-time category, but tonight it seemed she might have been wrong all along.

"This is delicious," Ryan said.

He must have meant it because he cleaned his plate. She'd forgotten how satisfying it was to cook a meal for someone who appreciated it. "Thanks."

"Maybe you should open that restaurant." Ryan rose and took his plate to the sink.

In the sudden, gaping silence, Ryan seemed to regret his words. "I'm sorry. I know times are hard for everyone. Every business owner in town is struggling." Vera winced. She could ski with the wind and cook like a chef. "I don't need your pity. The café is doing great."

"That's kind of what I thought. So tell me, why this urgency to get your hands on the top prize of twenty-five thousand dollars?" The penetrating look in his brown eyes almost undid her. But the pity in those eyes didn't sit well with her.

"What makes you think there's urgency? I didn't say any such thing." She rose to take her plate to the sink.

"Who decides on a whim to enter this kind of contest unless you desperately need the money?"

"I have never stepped down from a challenge." And she wasn't going to start now.

"I don't doubt that. But what if you don't win?

Have you considered that possibility?"

"Of course I have. I'm not an idiot." But in truth, if she didn't win this contest she would have to pick between her house and the café.

"But will you be OK without the winning purse?"

"Of course. Yeah, it would be nice. But contest or not, I'll be fine." She'd be all right, no matter what. Even if she had to bring in a cot to sleep in the café's office.

"I don't want to discourage you, but—" Ryan began.

"Then don't." She glared at him, hands on her hips, shoulders squared.

"You could get hurt." Ryan's gentle tone undid her again.

"Don't worry. I won't be a hero." Vera rolled her eyes.

"Ha, you're funny."

"If this is going to be a problem for you, I understand. I wouldn't want you to feel guilty about indulging me." She would almost like a way out of spending all this time with this irresistible man. Sometimes she swore he could see right through her.

"No. I don't mind training you. But I'll be tough.

It's what you'll need to beat the competition."

"I'm ready."

"You say that now, but I wonder how you'll feel after you've been through one of my training sessions at the gym."

"Gym?" She hated the gym. Didn't have a membership and didn't need one. The gym was a place fools frequented to torture themselves.

"Don't worry. I'm a card carrying member, and I'll get you in on a guest pass."

"Uh, what will we do at the gym?" She didn't like the sound of it. Not at all. There would probably be sweating involved at some point.

"What aren't we going to do at the gym?" Ryan smiled and cocked an eyebrow. "Push-ups, jumping jacks, the treadmill, the stair climber."

"Ryan, I should warn you. I don't do push-ups.

That's against my religion."

He actually laughed—a rolling and

hearty sound that made her heart skip. *Weird.*

"You'll have to be in the best shape of your life for this competition. If that's what you still plan on doing."

"Yes, but why the gym?"

Ryan held up his hand. "Don't argue with the trainer."

"All right. Whatever you say. Fascist," she muttered.

"You're right. This is now a dictatorship. If you want to be ready for the slopes, you need endurance."

They made plans to meet at Ryan's gym for the next two weeks leading up to the tournament. Every day seemed unreasonable, and though she argued her point, eventually Ryan won the argument with, among other things, his persuasive brown eyes.

RYAN STEPPED out of Vera's home and spotted the sleek dark vehicle parked near Vera's curb. Mr. Wall Street sat behind the wheel. No doubt watching Vera, but why?

He didn't know the guy's name yet, but the guy had earned stalker status in Ryan's book.

Ryan approached the shiny black Rolls Royce and tapped on its window.

Wall Street rolled down the window.

"Can I help you?" Ryan asked.

"Am I doing anything illegal, officer? I note you're not on duty by the lack of your uniform, but I'll excuse you for being over diligent. I know what it's like to love your job." He grinned with blindingly white teeth.

"Are you here to see Vera?" No more games with this creep.

"You might say that, but I'm waiting for the right time. I'm Kevin. Kevin Wright." He held out his hand.

Ryan shook Kevin's manicured, pale hand. "Ryan Colton. And how long did you plan on waiting for the right time?" Stalkers rarely wanted to volunteer any information, and until he knew better he would treat Kevin like one.

"Not much longer. Maybe I'll come back another time."

"Good idea."

"Timing is everything when it comes to Vera. Once you've been married to some-one, you remember these things."

"Married?" Experience taught him not

to take a stalker's word. Could Vera have ever been married to someone like this?

"That's right." He nodded.

"Regardless, that doesn't entitle you to spy on her from your car."

He laughed. "I'm hardly doing that. She'll be ready to talk soon."

"How's that?"

"Oh. You don't know. Well, Vera has gotten herself into quite a predicament. You know what that word means, right? She's in trouble. See, she's a little overextended. That means she doesn't have the cash flow to pay her bills. Do you understand? That happens in business sometimes."

"Overextended?" He'd let the guy treat him like an idiot as long as he kept on handing over information he could use.

"You may have noticed Vera likes the finer things in life. She certainly did during our marriage. People don't change. She'll never be happy until she gets herself out of this mess. And I can help."

"How can you help?" Ryan narrowed his eyes, waiting for what would come next.

"Do I have to spell it out for you?"

"Yeah, you might have to. You see, us public servants, we're a little dense."

"She may not realize it now, but Vera needs me. She needs the financial security I provide. I taught her everything she knows about business, and we make a pretty good team."

"How did she get overextended?" Ryan pressed.

"You should ask her," Kevin said.

"You can't park here all night." He slapped the hood of Kevin's car and hoped it annoyed the creep.

Kevin winced. "I wasn't planning on it."

"Yeah, see that you don't. In fact, why don't I follow you out of here? I'm sure you're done here now."

Ryan waited in his car. After a few seconds, Kevin started his vehicle and pulled away from the curb. Ryan followed him out of the neighborhood. So, Vera had entered the tournament for the purse. Challenge or not, she needed the money, even if she hadn't shared that with him.

Chapter 5

The gym met Vera's expectations. Men and women were equally clothed in her least favorite smell—sweat. The squeak of the treadmill as it circled round and round going nowhere, reminded her of the gerbils she had as a child. But her pets had no choice in the matter, while here, women and men raced on the treadmill going nowhere and paying good money to do it.

Worse, the air freshener did nothing to rid the building of the smell of dirty socks.

What was I thinking?

She'd tossed and turned all night imagining Kevin watched her as she slept, waiting for a chance to prove that she couldn't make it through this financial misstep without his help.

Who wouldn't have trouble sleeping with their creepy ex-husband sitting outside in his car?

Yeah, she'd seen him; she'd watched as Ryan spoke to him outside her home. She couldn't imagine what Kevin would say to Ryan, and that had kept her awake as well. One way or another she would find out what Kevin had told Ryan about her.

Now she was at the gym at 6:00 AM on a Sunday. The one day she could sleep in past the crack of dawn and she was trapped inside this building that dripped with testosterone. Without her morning cup of coffee, she fought sleep, but she planned to prove to Ryan that these workouts were not going to stop her.

"We better get going. I have to be at church at nine," Ryan said.

"Are you always here at this hour?" Vera searched for his faults. He sounded like a glutton for punishment. Strike one.

"I'm not usually here on a Sunday, but we have a tight schedule between your work hours and mine."

"So we won't always meet this early?"
Please. Say the words and make my day.

"Nope. Fortunately for us, the gym is open twenty four hours."

Vera stretched and yawned. He'd just made her

day.

The workout started with lunges and squats to

strengthen the legs. Once he made sure her legs felt like rubber, he had her run on the treadmill.

Like a torturer, Ryan kept increasing the speed until she sprinted and thought she would surely fall on her face.

"Stop." She changed the speed to a leisurely jog: four miles an hour.

Ryan changed it back to six miles per hour.

Dirty looks had no effect so she slapped his hand. His eyes widened and he grinned.

"Consider yourself lucky I only hit your hand," she said between breaths.

He climbed onto the treadmill next to hers, and she did her best to ignore him. Still, she couldn't help but notice that after five minutes, he barely broke a sweat. Until now, she hadn't noticed that he had abs, much less that they were rock hard.

"I happen to notice you speaking to someone who was parked in front of my house last night."

"Yeah. Same guy who was at the café." His words didn't come with the heavy breathing of someone taxed by a run.

Show off. Another flaw. She'd call that strike two.

"Kevin? What did he want?"

"He said he was your ex-husband."

"To my eternal shame."

Ryan didn't miss a beat. "Said he wanted to talk to you."

"Well, I don't want to talk to him."

If that was all Kevin had told him she'd consider herself fortunate.

"I got that idea." He slowed his speed and hopped off the treadmill. "Come on. We have a lot to do."

From treadmill to stair stepper. Running nowhere to climbing nowhere. What joy. The person who'd invented these machines had a wicked sense of humor. By the end of their session, the sweat dripped profusely from every pore she owned and surely some she didn't. Ryan threw a towel at her, and she slid down the length of the wall in a heap.

He was treating her like one of the guys. Why, then, did she hate it?

"Good work. Tomorrow we'll step it up a little. I didn't want to be too hard on you the first day."

Kyle ambled over to them, a sly grin on his face and a towel around his shoulders. He held out his hand to Vera and pulled her up. "I see you mean to give me some serious competition."

"You better believe it." Vera caught her breath.

She hadn't noticed Kyle at the gym. Now she was glad Ryan had put her through the paces, and she'd kept up. Since she'd proven herself to Ryan, Kyle might take her seriously, too. She stood straighter and tried to still the rubber she used to refer to as her legs.

"It takes a lot more than a few gym workouts to make you a pro, sweetheart. Don't let this joker tell you otherwise." Kyle snapped his towel at Ryan.

Ryan's jaw flexed, but he ignored Kyle and stared at Vera. "You did great."

"If you ever want a ski lesson from a real

pro, I'll clear my schedule." Kyle was handsome in a gold- chain, hairy-chest way, and her skin crawled when he spoke.

"No thanks." Vera staggered toward the exit sign. All she could think of was a shower and an industrial size cup of coffee. If only her legs could hold her up.

She'd made it through the workout. If Ryan thought he would discourage her, he would have to come up with Plan B. They would all be shocked at what she could do when she put her mind to it.

RYAN WANTED to wipe the leer off Kyle's face. Kyle's intentions weren't honorable, Ryan was certain. "How did you get in here, anyway?"

"Ashley gave me a guest pass. It's the least she can do since I make her breakfast every morning." Kyle winked.

Just as Ryan suspected. "Great. And you can lay off Vera," he warned Kyle as he grabbed his backpack off the floor.

Kyle ogled as Vera walk toward the exit sign.

"Why? Are you interested in her?"

Even if he was, he wouldn't tell Kyle.

That knowledge would ring like a challenge to Kyle.

"You're the last thing she needs right now."

"Are you sure, bud?" Kyle narrowed his eyes.

"Yeah. Don't play your games with her."

"That's not what I meant. Are you sure *you're* not interested in her?"

Beautiful, brave, and funny. Smart. Vera had everything going for her, but he'd promised himself he wouldn't ask anyone out again until it could be a serious relationship. No more fooling around. And Vera had some kind of anti-religion agenda that he didn't quite understand.

Especially since she was best friends with Maggie, who was as Christian a girl as one could ever meet.

"If you're not interested I might be." Kyle shrugged. "I'm just saying."

Vera needed someone like Kyle in her life the way the gym needed more sweat. "Even if there's a jealous ex-husband involved?"

Kyle's smile fell. Jealous ex-husbands happened to be a personal problem of Kyle's, and there had been plenty of them, if the rumors were true. Kyle's silence provided his answer.

"See you tomorrow. We're training every day." Ryan turned to leave. He spied the backpack Vera had left behind. He carted it out.

Vera stood by her car plundering through her purse. "I know I had keys or I couldn't have driven myself here."

"You forgot something." He handed her the gym bag.

She snatched it from his hands, fumbled through it, and fished out a set of keys. "I'm not sure if I'm speaking to you yet. You're some kind of sadist." Vera narrowed her eyes.

"Once you take a hot shower, you'll feel like a new woman. You'll see."

"If you say so."

"I do. See you tomorrow?"

"Not if I see you first." She punched her key.

The lock clicked, and he opened the door for her.

"C'mon. You used to be a model. Didn't they want you to keep in shape with regular workouts?"

Vera laughed. "A water and lettuce diet doesn't give you much energy for workouts."

He knew next to nothing about the fashion industry, but no one in their right mind could expect to survive on a diet of lettuce and water. "Tell me you're kidding."

"I'm only exaggerating a little. Why do you think I like to eat so much now?'

One could hardly tell by looking at her, but she'd certainly eaten a lot of pasta the night before, and it did seem a fitting tribute to enjoy food once you had been severely deprived of it.

"Go home and eat a huge protein-laden breakfast.

You earned it."

"That's the wisest thing you've said to me this morning. I might be speaking to you again."

He tried to keep a straight face, but Vera made him want to smile.

The financial problems were serious enough that she wasn't backing off even with his punitive workouts. He'd tested her this morning to see how determined she was, and giving up didn't seem to be part of her vocabulary.

Whatever the financial problem, it had

to be significant. But how would he get her to admit it so he could help in a real way?

The men's Bible study group had picked John chapter two for study. The first miracle of turning water into wine.

Bible study helped Ryan make practical applications for daily life, but today he wondered how he could possibly apply this passage. Water and wine.

Could this be about making the best of a bad situation?

Ex-Sheriff Calhoun, the eldest in the group, spoke first. "I see this as Mary stating the problem: they had no more wine. At a wedding in the first century, that was a huge problem."

"That's always a problem. First century or not," a younger man quipped from the back row.

"Well, I give you that," Calhoun continued. "Mary put the problem to Jesus, and then she trusted in Him to solve it. I'm not even sure she realized this would be His first public miracle."

"So, basically, state the problem and then wait and trust in God," Ryan said. Made sense. Ryan marveled at how Calhoun found bits of wisdom from the smallest things.

"Exactly. He knows what's on our minds so we might as well be honest," Jack added.

They ended with prayer in time to make it to the second service in the main chapel. During his own prayer, Ryan took the time to present the problem: Vera's financial difficulty and his desire to help her with it.

Ryan walked out with Jack and Calhoun.

Maggie and Lexi were coming out of the church nursery where they'd both volunteered.

Ryan hugged Maggie. She was about ready to burst with child. Although she'd always been pretty, now she looked almost ethereal.

"I've been meaning to call you. We keep missing each other at church." She let Jack and Lexi walk ahead.

"What's up?"

"I'm hoping that Vera came to see you?"

He didn't think Maggie knew that he had offered to train Vera for the tournament. "We started training today. I took her to the slopes a couple of days ago."

Maggie's eyes widened. "Training?"

"For the open ski tournament. She insists on entering." He shrugged.

Maggie shook her head. "I told Vera about the foundation. She has one of those interest only loans, and she can't afford the payment any longer. I gave her a brochure and told her to call and find out more about it."

So that was the financial problem. The reason she was overextended. If she'd told him about it, they could have avoided this tournament business. The foundation was there to help people like Vera.

"I don't know why she hasn't asked you about it. She said she would. But knowing Vera, she's probably too proud."

"Crazy." Ryan's jaw tightened. "Instead, she's entered a ski tournament with highly ranked amateurs and professionals. And she's got a ways to go to be in the same league. I don't think she stands a chance, but more than that, I'm worried she could get hurt."

"Oh, no." Maggie covered her face with her hands.

Ryan was sorry he'd told her anything. "You've got to convince her to take the assistance."

"I'll try, but this is some kind of challenge to her. She hasn't given me any hints of backing down." If her best friend couldn't convince Vera to ask for help, how was he supposed to make any headway?

"It won't be easy, but take it from my experience.

Eventually, she does listen to reason."

The Vera he'd been working with hadn't seemed all that familiar with reason. But now, at last, he knew exactly how to help her. He'd have to bring it up tactfully and let her know he realized this race wasn't just a challenge to her, but a real need. One which the foundation could cure. If only she'd listen to him.

THE HARDEST THING Vera had found thus far about being Maggie's best friend turned out to be planning the baby shower.

She'd handled offering Maggie advice during Lexi's rough patch a few years ago because she understood a little something about teenage rebellion.

But when it came to babies she couldn't offer anything. Babies were far too fragile for Vera's sensibilities. Too helpless. And the memory of her greatest failure as a human being. But she'd leave that in the past where it belonged. She had to drum up some enthusiasm for Maggie's sake because she had invitations to send out today.

After the gym torture, Vera ate a large breakfast of eggs mixed with bits of bacon, sausage, and potatoes. She handed Stin a small piece of bacon. "Don't tell the vet."

A long and luxurious shower proved Ryan was right. She felt normal again.

She had finished addressing the last of the invitations to the baby shower by hand and risen to stretch out her legs when her gaze caught a byline in the Harte's Peak Times that sat on her kitchen counter.

In the Lifestyle section, an article on the upcoming ski tournament at Dodge Ridge listed the names of all contestants, including her own.

The First Annual Dodge Ridge Open Ski Tournament, sponsored by Columbia under the direction of the Harte's Peak Chamber of Commerce, promises to be a popular event. Next month, amateur ranked and professional skiers from Colorado to Utah will compete for the top prize of $25,000. A series of races before the tournament will determine whether the amateur can advance to *the final. A professional ranking guarantees advancement.*

The names of the entrants and their short bios were listed. A long list of titles and awards followed Kyle's name and the names of the other competitors. Shane Zelinski was a highly ranked amateur, one qualifying race from the pro-circuit and was second favored to win after Kyle. Ryan was right. Even all the amateurs listed had prior experience in tournament skiing.

Except for her. Vera's credentials were listed as a resident of Harte's Peak and owner of The Bean Café. Her past high fashion modeling experience didn't matter.

The black and white typeset invited second thoughts. Sure, she could ski, but so could Ryan. So could Jack, Lexi, and almost every one of her friends. It didn't mean that they could enter a ski tournament. They were at least smart enough to realize that.

What had she done?

Maybe she could still drop out and keep some dignity, although the damage was already done. Suddenly Kyle didn't seem as egotistical as she'd thought. It was a wonder he hadn't laughed her right out of the gym. He was probably humoring her. Big mistake.

And Ryan—-no wonder he had tried so hard to talk her out of it. Looking back, he'd been kind.

Shutting her eyes, she took a deep and calming breath. Maybe if she went out for a while and took her mind off it, she'd gain a fresh perspective. She still hadn't found the perfect gift for Maggie—one in Vera's price range.

The phone rang, and she picked it up expecting to hear Maggie in shock after reading the paper. She'd probably cry until Vera gave in and dropped out.

"You can't be serious." Kevin said, with a jovial tone.

"What do you want?" she snapped.

"I'm reading the local paper, and I come across this article that states in no uncertain terms that my ex- wife is about to participate in a ski tournament she doesn't have a prayer of winning. Is this your plan to get out from under your obligations?"

"What possible business is this of yours?" She held the phone tightly, considering whether she should hang up on him or throw the phone across the room.

"Whether you believe it or not, I care about you. If this is your plan, I'm worried.

Did you read the article and assess your competition? Didn't I teach you better than this?"

"Kevin, do me a favor and lose this number." She hit the button to hang up.

She needed to get out of the house and go shopping to take her mind off the tournament.

As the best friend she wanted to buy Maggie the most expensive item on the register, a state-of-the-art stroller. But she might have to squash that generous spirit since her bank account didn't line up with her motives. She'd made a partial payment to her mortgage lender hoping to appease them, though she doubted it would do much to delay the inevitable. At this point, the tournament couldn't get here fast enough, if it was going to make any difference at all.

She'd exhausted her savings and broken the cardinal rule to dip into the small retirement fund she'd started. None of it would be enough to dig her out of this hole. The house payment was eating her alive.

The house wasn't even worth what she still owed to the bank. In business terms, it would be considered a loss and she should write it off. But this was her home and Stin's home, too. It couldn't be written off like some item in an accountant's liability column.

She glanced down at Stin, her little shadow. Some apartments might take pets, but she didn't want Stin cramped up in a small place with no yard.

The place that used to offer her such comfort, with its large kitchen island perfect for cooking, now threatened to strangle her from the inside out.

Vera grabbed her keys to drive over to Wee Ones and find out exactly how much that stroller Maggie wanted would cost.

She pulled up into the parking lot of the small store and held her breath. The last time she'd been here was with Maggie, but now she'd have to walk in alone. She hated this place with its aisles of broken promises. Pictures of angelic looking babies everywhere, plump faced and healthy looking, the way all babies should be.

Blanche was more than happy to oblige when she asked about the stroller, looking it up on the baby register Maggie had signed up for a week ago.

"Still available." Blanche checked. "No one purchased it yet."

Vera stared at the tag. No wonder.

Like a woman possessed, Vera whipped out her credit card. "I'll get it."

Maggie deserved it. Buying it would demonstrate to Maggie how much she loved her. How much she missed working with her at the café every day.

Blanche came back with the card. "It didn't go through. Want me to try again?"

Vera's stomach dropped. They'd obviously lowered her credit limit, since she hadn't hit the maximum limit on her *emergency only* credit card.

Blanche stared at her and waited for an answer.

"Oh," Vera managed to say. There were no more credit cards. There would be no stroller for Maggie. Not from her anyway.

She turned and marched out of the store without saying another word.

Blanche kept calling her name.

Vera ignored her. In her car, she sat and stared straight ahead. Babies were bad luck for her. Bad luck fourteen years ago and tough luck now.

Two doors down from Wee Ones stood the ski equipment store, Xtreme Ski. One shop illustrated her past failures, the other

her future ones. The chances she would win this tournament were non-existent.

Eight years ago, she'd shed the last of her tears, and there should be no need to start again now. She'd get through this. She'd survived a lot worse and this bump only meant a smoother road lay ahead.

Only this time the internal pep talk didn't work. Big wet tears rolled down her cheeks without restraint, followed by a rumbling that began somewhere inside her gut and forced her to heave and shake against her will.

When she thought to look at the clock on her dashboard, an hour had passed. She'd sat in her car alone and sobbed for an hour. And yet more tears kept coming. This must be what happens when you let it build up.

She glanced up at a tap on her window.

Outside her car, Ryan stared with a furrowed brow.

Chapter 6

Ryan waited.

The door clicked as Vera unlocked it.

Without speaking, he opened it and pulled her out of the car and into his arms.

She buried her face in his shoulder without complaint. She felt too thin in his arms and he worried he'd crush her. Her hair felt like spun silk in his rough hands as he stroked it gently and rubbed her back.

"Who did this to you?" He wanted to know. He'd hurt the guy. Well, now that he was a Christian he couldn't hurt him, but he could scare him off. As far as he knew, there wasn't anything in the Bible about that.

Vera hiccuped and tried to catch her

breath, which almost tore his heart from his chest. "What do you mean?"

"It's that jerk, Kevin, isn't it? Just tell me what he did, Vera, and I'll take care of it." He tried to breathe through his anger. He didn't want to scare her.

Vera pulled away and put her hands over her face.

"He didn't do anything."

"I find that hard to believe. What does he want?" Time to admit the truth. He'd like to know the reason Kevin hung around a slow poke town like theirs. It couldn't be the weather, because by the looks of that Rolls Royce, it had never seen any snow or sleet before. She avoided his eyes. "He wants to buy the café.

That's what he wants. And since that would make me miserable, it's kind of an added bonus."

"Why would a Wall Street type like him want to buy your cafe?" It sounded like the ex wanted to help, as he'd told Ryan. Obviously, Vera didn't want his help, and he couldn't blame her. That cafe was her life blood, her passion

"To take it away from me."

"But you don't have to sell it to him. Last time I checked it's a free country."

"I don't have to, and I won't. But I need the money. I'm behind on my mortgage payments since they doubled three months ago. I can't keep up anymore."

"That's why you're entering the tournament." Finally she'd admitted the truth to him. Now he could talk to her freely about the foundation.

"Now you know. Happy?"

"I wish you'd told me first. I can help." Without a second thought, he put his hands on her shoulders.

"No, Ryan. I don't want help from the foundation. I didn't want to tell you why I needed this money because I knew you would bring that up. Use the foundation's help for someone else. I can find a way out of this even if the ski tournament doesn't work out. And you and I both know I'm a long shot."

The defeat in her voice shook him. "Are you thinking of dropping out now?"

"Of course not." Vera shook her head.

No, that would make sense. "Then what?"

"I'll do my best, and if I don't win, maybe I'll have to let the bank take it back."

"I assume you tried to sell it?"

"And what I could get for it in today's market won't cover what I owe." "You'll lose everything you put into it."

"All that remodeling. I should have listened to my mother, the miser, not my sister, the interior designer."

"This is crazy, Vera. Why won't you accept help from the foundation?" Hands still on her shoulders, he resisted the urge to shake some sense into her.

"Save it for the people who need it. Maybe the people who show up for church every Sunday. After all, they've earned it."

Ryan tensed and took a step back. "It's not about earning it. We want to help the community."

"You want to tell people about Jesus. Well, save it. Jesus and I are fine; it's His people that I'm not particularly fond of."

"What's that supposed to mean?" His jaw felt tight enough to break a molar.

"You can't brush on a new coat of paint and tell me that you've changed."

"But I have." His eyes narrowed. "This

isn't a fresh, new coat of paint. It's a remodeling job from the inside out."

"Enough with the home improvement metaphors." She rolled her eyes.

"You started it." He shrugged.

"You can't change who you are." She stared at him.

"Maybe not, but with Christ you can become the best version."

"Fine, so you're a better version of the playboy who used to ask me out once a week. The one who asked my best friend out, too."

Ouch. The look on her face told Ryan that she'd resented being one of many. He looked at the ground.

"You could say that, but I'm not a playboy, anymore. I haven't dated anyone since I became a Christian."

"Not enough nice Christian girls out there? Was Maggie the last good one?"

"I'm sure they're plenty. I'm not looking for anyone. I have to work on myself first."

"You're serious?" She narrowed her eyes.

"Like a heart attack. And this foundation is our chance to put our faith into action. We don't just want to talk about helping people.

We're actually trying to do something for the community."

"Good for you. What do you want, a medal?"

"I want you to stop being so stubborn and at least consider how the foundation could help. You don't even know how it works. You haven't taken the time to find out."

"I don't want to be a charity case." She raised her chin.

"But—"

"I'm not talking about it anymore." She folded her arms and looked at the ground.

Darn this stubborn woman. She drove him crazy. The answer was right in front of her eyes, and she couldn't see it.

"At least think about it." He could be stubborn, too.

Sooner or later Vera would come around to his way of thinking. He had to be patient, continue the workouts, and wait her out.

As for Kevin, the man obviously wanted to take away something precious to Vera. If he wanted to help he'd pay off the amount she owed and allow her to catch up. But apparently, he had his own agenda. That much was clear.

Ryan decided to keep an eye on the jerk and make sure he didn't hurt Vera.

And he recalled Vera's declaration. "Jesus and I are fine." She'd never talked about her faith. There had to have been something in her past that changed her mind about God's people.

Although he'd seen his share of Sunday hypocrites, most of the members in attendance at his church were the real thing. If Vera got to know them as he had, she would give them a chance.

He'd been toying with an idea in the back of his mind since Vera launched this crazy plan to enter the tournament. And even though the idea still made him break out in a cold sweat, he'd work through the panic. He would have to for Vera's sake.

His faith would have to be strong enough to get him through the memories of the accident. He'd prayed about it, and after today, the answer seemed clear.

More than anyone, Vera had a desperate need to win, and now, he had an even better idea of how to help her.

· · ·

VERA DROVE HOME after assuring Ryan that the public would be safe with her behind the wheel. The sob fest had actually been cathartic, as though her tears had a healing quality in them. Next time, she'd have to make sure to cry in private.

Still, the memory of Ryan's arms around her warmed her heart. He didn't look like a man who hugged as well as he did. She sighed at the memory of how tenderly he'd held her and how safe she'd felt in his embrace.

He smelled like a man–leather, soap, and after shave. *Do not go there, Vera.* Especially not now, not with this new Ryan. He didn't run in the other direction of a hysterical woman, so either this was some type of new game he played, or perhaps he did qualify for sainthood.

Now that he realized Kevin was her ex, he didn't seem to judge her for that mistake. Perhaps it was because he had a past full of his own mistakes. She was curious as to why he wouldn't talk about the accident. He kept that part of himself a mystery. She wanted to know, but she had too much respect for him to go behind his back and ask Kyle or Jack.

Ryan would tell her eventually. Or she'd wear him down.

One thing she would never believe was that a man was good simply because he graced the entrance of a church. No, Kevin had proved that loud and clear. He'd been a leader at the church when they'd lived in Texas after getting married. He'd fooled her and everyone else. A business leader in the community, too.

He'd fooled Mom, too.

Looking back, maybe she should have told her mother the truth. Told her that Kevin had cheated. Not once or twice, but repeatedly.

In the end Kevin had taken something she didn't think anyone could: her faith. He'd done that when he'd convinced the members of the congregation that she'd been the one to violate the marriage vows, not him. And they'd believed him. It might have been what they expected from a former fashion model. The memory of that abandonment as they took Kevin's side in their divorce still pained her. And it was the reason she hadn't been to church except on holidays, when there didn't seem to be much choice.

But Ryan was different. He was beginning to remind her that not all men were the same. Since that day long ago when she'd seen the new deputy stop traffic so that a little boy could catch his dog, Ryan Colton had caught her attention.

Even then, something inside her cold heart had stirred. A man who loved animals couldn't be all bad. But Ryan had proved himself to be a playboy shortly after that, asking both her and Maggie out in the same week.

Maybe he had changed. They'd been alone together in her home, and he hadn't even tried to kiss her. And now, today, at her most vulnerable, he only provided the comfort of a warm and dry shoulder.

Ryan would never understand, though, why she couldn't take money from the foundation. That would require an explanation beyond what she was capable of giving to him. And it would require a forgiveness she doubted anyone could give. Not even Ryan.

Two days later Vera waited outside of the lodge after checking in. She pinned her lift ticket to her pink and black ski jacket. The tournament entrants were given free lift tickets, a specially marked stub that read

"Contestant."

Ryan greeted her as he arrived and went inside. When he returned, he was wearing a "contestant" ticket stub.

"What's that?" She pointed at the stub on his brown jacket. "Are they letting everyone have one of those today?"

"Nope." Ryan pulled on his gloves.

He didn't volunteer any information, and she tried to contain her curiosity.

"I entered the open just in time to qualify. Barely made the deadline. Isn't that something?" He smiled as he tapped the stub on his ski jacket.

"You're supposed to be training me. Did you forget our agreement? Now you're my competition."

He hadn't changed, not deep inside. Now he would pull out all the stops, show off every one of his techniques and demonstrate his superior skill on the trails.

"Calm down. I'm still training you. Turns out I'm getting my ski legs back by helping you out."

"You're not helping me out. You just pushed me out of the running."

Ryan pulled her to the side.

"Listen, I've increased your odds of winning."

"Really, Einstein? And how is that?"

"Because if I qualify and make it to the finals and win, I'll give you the money. If you qualify and win you get the money. Seems to be an increase in odds there."

"But I told you I didn't want you to do that. I want to do this."

"And you are. But so am I. Listen. I can't stop you from entering, but you can't stop me either. Are we clear?"

She stared. Had he improved her chances? Winning might actually be in her sights now. "We're clear. As long as it's on record that I didn't ask you to do this."

He laughed. "Is it that hard for you to accept help from a friend?"

"Yes." She shrugged.

But she couldn't wait to see the look on Kyle's face when he realized that Ryan had entered. She could tell the two of them had a real competitive streak between them.

She continued to stare at him in silence. Vera didn't know what else to say to this man. He wouldn't stop surprising her. A man who would hand over twenty-five thousand dollars to her because she needed it more than he did. Was it even possible?

"Let's get going." Carrying his skis, Ryan walked in the direction of the ski lift and she followed.

Over the next four hours, they went on several runs together and she kept up with Ryan's speed easily. But she also noticed several things—he had so much more control than she did. He never lost his footing, whereas a couple of times she had.

One of those times Ryan skied past her, but looked back. He stopped his run to help her.

"What did I tell you about going so fast without control?"

"You said not to do it." His racing past had annoyed her since he supposedly hadn't skied in years. Ryan crouched down to check her bindings and boots. "I'm not sure this is the best fit for you.

Sometimes it's about the equipment. You need a solid foundation."

She'd foundation him if he didn't give up on the subtle hints. His nearness distracted her, and she slapped his hand away from her boot.

"I can do it." She tightened the bindings.

Finished, she looked up to see him staring at her, an amused smile on his face.

"Yes, you can. But you can let me help sometimes."

Vera bit her lip. "I'm trying."

"I know that, darlin'."

After a few more words from Ryan extolling the virtues of control, they were off again.

The wind whipped across her cheeks, and she joined Ryan as side by side they conquered the mountain.

Chapter 7

Ryan sat with Vera at her cafe after a long day on the slopes.

As expected, Kyle's eyes had narrowed like slits when he noticed Ryan's new ski lift tag denoting him as a fellow competitor.

"Did you see the look on Kyle's face?" Vera laughed.

"He looked evil." Ryan wouldn't let Kyle know he was not in it for himself. That would take all the fun out of it. He also wasn't going to share with Vera that he fought panic every time he pushed off, because she might feel guilty. He'd handle the fear with the Lord's help.

Ryan was riding high because Vera had

finally accepted his help. Even if she rejected the foundation, and he hoped that would change, she'd let down her guard enough to not stop him from helping.

And now he was enjoying the best coffee in town, on the house.

"Kyle knows you're his only real competition." Vera leaned in across the table from Ryan.

Ryan wanted to believe that, but it wasn't true. Kyle had stayed on the circuit. Ryan hadn't looked back—until Vera needed him.

"I guess things will be rather tense. He'll get over
it."

Vera's blue eyes shone and the light sound of her voice lifted his spirits. He still hadn't shaken how her sobs had torn away at places in his heart.

"Have you ever beaten him before?" Vera took a sip of her coffee.

"There was this one time in Utah—the Park City Ski Town Shoot Out. To be fair, he did have a bad day, but I came in first."

"I bet he never forgot that one."

"Of course he excused it by claiming an old knee injury reared its ugly head. Who knows? Maybe it was even true. Usually, I came in a close second. But you never know."

"You're good on those slopes. Really good. What made you quit?"

"Always wanted to be a cop. Ever since I was a little kid playing cops and robbers."

"Ever the robber?"

"Never or I wouldn't play."

Annie watched them from behind the counter.

Vera had her working more shifts so she could spend more time training.

To Annie and everyone else, he and Vera probably seemed like a couple. Hopefully, his old reputation wouldn't taint hers.

"Believe it or not, as a kid I thought I would join the military." Vera looked past him, her blue eyes misty.

"You? In the military? You are aware you have to take orders there?"

She smirked. "I wanted to get away from my mother. But just when I thought I couldn't take it anymore, a modeling scout found me when we were traveling in Paris."

"That's when you started modeling?" He'd always wondered about that part of her life. She never talked about it.

"I was young. You would think that the mother of a seventeen-year-old might want her daughter chaperoned, but not mine."

"She let you go off by yourself?" He knew exactly how protective Jack and Maggie were over their teenaged daughter, Lexi. And for good reason, in his opinion.

"She did." Vera nodded. "I thought it was great at the time. I was finally out from under her control. Sure, I missed my sister, but I didn't miss my mother. She has a way of serving up extra bitterness with morning tea. But in Europe, I was on my own. I had my tea with sugar, hold the bitter."

"But it wasn't a good thing in the long run."

"Not at all. That was how I met him." Vera gazed down, as though she was recalling something shameful.

"Who?"

"Kevin. If I'd had a chaperone, it might have been harder to cut through my defenses. But—"

"You were only seventeen?" His back stiffened.

What kind of creep went after a teenager?

"I was nineteen, by then. Traveled

around the world and thought I knew something. Thought I was sophisticated. Worldly. Ha." Vera gazed outside to the light snowfall of late January. "He was older than me by fourteen years. Very successful and confident. He had money and influence. He took my career to the next level. And then he ran it into the ground, just because he could."

"Why?" He spoke softly, afraid she would realize she was opening up to him.

"To control me, I guess. So I retired from modeling, came home, and tried to be a good wife and business partner. We went to church together. We built our real estate business. And he worked to cut everyone else out of my life."

"Your family?"

"He was the liaison between my mother and me, had been since he met me. But then he didn't want me to talk to my sister, Amy. Maybe he thought she would talk some sense into me."

"Did she?"

"Yes. When she finally came to see me against his wishes and found me thinner than I'd been on the runway. Sick and pale. She told me that no matter what other people thought of Kevin, he was obviously not taking care of me." She shrugged.

"What happened?"

"I didn't leave right away, but then I found out he had been unfaithful to me, and when I told him I knew, he denied it. I asked him to stop. To give our marriage a chance. I tried to get him to go to counseling, but he wouldn't listen. I tried to make it work, Ryan, but I had no choice. To this day my mother doesn't get it. She's clueless. She won't understand that I tried. But Kevin, in his controlling way, wanted both worlds, and when I wouldn't hear of it…" She stared off into the corner.

"Anyway, that's why I stopped going to church."

"Because of Kevin?"

She nodded. "He convinced our church leaders that I'd been the bad wife, that I'd had the affairs and chosen to end the marriage. Kevin has a big personality, and he ambushes people who are trusting and open-hearted."

"They blamed you?"

"They sided with Kevin. I felt abandoned. A divorce is always difficult, but particularly when you lose your support system."

Ryan's body tensed. He'd not trusted Kevin from the beginning. "I don't know what to say, except that you deserved better than that."

"Don't feel too sorry for me. I got a generous settlement in the divorce. Courtesy of a good attorney, not Kevin. But it allowed me to start over here in Harte's Peak, buy my own home. And buy this café." She looked around as though she was watching a child who had grown up too fast.

His heart clenched.

Vera might lose everything. She'd already started over once before. It wasn't fair.

"Vera, you won't lose your house or your livelihood." Not if he had anything to do with it.

She smiled with such warmth that heat settled in and around places inside his heart. *Don't go there, Ryan. Don't get ahead of yourself.*

Only a few stragglers remained in the café, and Annie closed up the register when he got up to leave. He didn't want to, but he had the late shift.

"I'll walk you out." Vera followed him

outside to the parking lot and stood next to his truck.

"Tomorrow at the gym. Meet you at five."

She nodded and then unexpectedly brought her arms up around his shoulders and hugged him tightly.

"Thank you," she whispered the words in his ear.

His arms went around her waist, and he pulled her closer. Today she smelled like vanilla. Forgetting himself, he traced the curve of her face, finding impossibly soft skin. Until now, he hadn't realized her beauty ran much more than skin deep.

So much more.

Annie, observing through the pane glass window, jerked him out of his daze and he let Vera go. He didn't want to start anything he couldn't finish.

Vera's vulnerability showed in every angle of her porcelain-like face. What she needed right now was a friend.

And he resolved to be that friend.

As the days passed, filled with agonizing trips to the gym and exhilarating days on the mountain, Vera grew used to Ryan, growing comfortable with his opening the doors for her, holding out a hand every time she fell, and never missing a chance to talk about the foundation.

Rather than annoy her as it had in the beginning, she found it endearing that the man would not give up. And even though it meant he had less time for his own runs he gave her pointers every day.

In two days, she'd face her qualifying race. They both would.

Ryan had a much better chance than she did, but warmth spread in her because the two of them were a team.

When it came time for Maggie's baby shower, Vera took the day off from training, her first since she'd started this pursuit of the purse.

The college tour Maggie's daughter, Lexi, had planned conflicted with her mother's baby shower. Lexi was a little disappointed, but she'd made the trip with Jack.

Vera arrived with the cake as Lexi's grandmother, Paula, was repositioning a table.

"Good. The cake is here. Put it in there, dear." Paula directed her to the kitchen.

Vera found Maggie sitting on the stool in the kitchen, dark circles under her eyes. "I'm trying to stay out of their way. I've had a backache all day and I'm already exhausted. Good timing, huh?"

"Rest and enjoy yourself. You're to do nothing else today, but receive presents and eat." Vera opened the refrigerator and set the cake inside.

"I can't wait for Jack and Lexi to come back. I miss them so much already." Maggie sniffed. Since getting pregnant, it was not uncommon for Maggie to cry during commercials for kitty litter. .

"When will they be back?"

"Their flight home leaves tomorrow morning." Maggie reached for a potato chip from the trays of snacks on the counter.

"How does Lexi like the college?"

Maggie had already expressed her fear that her daughter would move across the country to attend school. "Apparently, she loves it," Maggie said, sounding as if she delivered a eulogy.

"Don't look so sad. It's not written in stone. Something tells me she'll want to be nearby to dote on her little brother." She rubbed Maggie's back.

Vera's gift, two packages of diapers, sat in the trunk of her car. She couldn't face bringing them in yet. Vera wanted to buy something better, but according to her sister, diapers were the best gift one could give a new parent. For now, they'd have to do.

If she won this tournament, or if Ryan did, she'd buy Maggie a much better gift. Not that it would make any difference to Maggie.

"I'm supposed to talk some sense into you," Maggie said.

"About what?"

"The tournament. What's gotten into you? It sounds too dangerous."

"Ryan told you about the race?" What else had he told Maggie?

"I saw him at church, and he assumed I already knew. But why didn't you tell me?"

"Maybe because I knew you'd try to talk me out of it?" Of all the differences between her and Maggie, their risk tolerance was the greatest.

"Ryan asked me to do that, and I hoped you'd listen to reason," Maggie said.

"He's still trying to do that? I thought he'd given up. I wish both of you would have a little more faith in my abilities." Vera frowned.

"It's not that. I've never even known you

to ski. You told me the last time you had was during that photo shoot in Telluride. That was years ago. You showed me photos, remember?"

"So what? It came back to me like I thought it would."

"Enough to compete with those pros?" Maggie's face flushed, and for a moment, Vera regretted that she had any part in the tension written there.

"I'll manage."

"You're asking a lot of a woman in my condition, but something tells me I'll spend the next couple of days on my knees." Maggie shuffled a bit on the stool.

"Thank you." She'd take Maggie's prayers any day of the week.

"So how is the training going?" Maggie switched to full-on support mode and Vera breathed a sigh of relief.

"The gym is not my favorite place, and it never will be, but it's grown on me. And Ryan has been great, I have to admit." More than great. Kind of dreamy, actually. Yesterday she had been sure he'd wanted to kiss her. But he must have thought twice about that. She'd told him all about her sordid past. A guy like Ryan needed a good woman and that certainly wasn't her.

Vera's phone rang. She excused herself and pulled it out of her purse.

"Ms. Carrington? This is Sally Wentworth from the Home is Where the Heart Is Foundation. Your name came up on our list and we can start the process as soon as we get your application and lender information."

"List? What list?"

"The list of applicants who need assistance," Sally said.

Vera's cheeks burned. She could feel the heat spread all the way down to her toes. "I don't know where you got your information, but I didn't apply to any list. There must be some mistake."

"I don't think so. It's right here. Someone put you on the list." Sally spelled out Vera's name and gave her home address. She had the right person. "So, do you still need the assistance or not?"

She couldn't speak for several seconds. "I'll call you back." Vera threw her cell phone back in her purse.

Ryan. The nerve of that man. He'd completely disregarded what she wanted and added her to the list. She counted to ten and tried to calm down. This wasn't the time or the place. She'd deal with Ryan soon enough.

Maggie had moved and now sat in Jack's recliner chair. A gutsy move, because it might be hard for her to get out of it.

The guests arrived and before long, the party was in full swing with a large crowd of friends.

Vera was in charge of the games and there were plenty of silly ones to play. Katie, from the bookstore, had directed her to a book with several great ideas.

The time to open gifts arrived, and true to form, Paula had purchased the expensive stroller. At least Maggie had what she wanted. Even Vera's gift of diapers was well received.

After the cake was served, everyone gradually started to file out and leave tired Maggie alone to rest. The party had drained her. Her face looked flushed and sweaty.

Paula left after helping Vera take down all the decorations and clean up the kitchen.

"I can stay if you want."

"I'm afraid you have to. I think I'm in labor." Maggie winced. "Help me up."

"Not funny. The party games are over." Vera offered a hand and pulled Maggie out of the recliner.

"I'm not kidding. How I wish I was. Jack's not going to be here." She started to cry.

"It's too soon, isn't it? Can't you do something?"

"What exactly do you expect me to do?" Maggie asked, still sniffling as tears ran down her cheeks.

"I don't know, but there has to be something."

"Nothing will stop the baby from coming," Maggie groaned, and the sound startled Vera. Oh mercy, she was serious.

But premature babies did not do well and even though the size of Maggie's stomach indicated she had a full grown one in there, how could anyone know for certain that the baby would be healthy?

Calm down. Breathe.

"But I don't know what to do." Vera fought to keep the panic out of her voice.

"Take me to the hospital, dummy." Maggie moaned and clutched her stomach.

Of course, she could do that. In fact, she could do it quickly. Finally, a legitimate reason to speed through town. "I thought the baby wasn't due for another four weeks." She opened the back door of her car and eased Maggie inside.

"No one told him. He will probably be ornery like his father," Maggie said.

"Someone should have told him," Vera mumbled under her breath even as she realized that it made no sense. She got behind the wheel and hoped that the vehicle would be able to rise to the challenge. She'd observed the speed limit since she'd traded down, so she wasn't sure how fast it could go.

Tonight they would all find out.

As she ramped up the speed, she fully expected Maggie to tell her to slow down. She revved the engine up to sixty-five on the narrow country road, a dangerous attempt for an inexperienced driver, but she could handle it.

Maggie groaned from the back, "Hurry!"

Oh, no, her best friend, who always followed the rules, wanted her to go faster. The sound of despair in Maggie's voice caused a chill to run down Vera's back. She floored it.

Like clockwork, the siren blared loudly and the bright lights flashed.

"Sorry, Maggie. I have to stop." Of all the times to get pulled over.

"Do it!" Maggie screamed. "You can get a police escort."

Why hadn't she thought of that? Probably because Ryan was on duty and she was still too angry to speak to him. It would be difficult not to give him a piece of her mind. He shouldn't have called the foundation on her behalf. He should have respected her wishes.

She pulled over and jumped out of the car to meet Ryan.

"Vera, what are you thinking?" he asked. "Do you have any idea how fast you were going?"

"Maggie's in the backseat, and she's about to have her baby. I need to get to the hospital. Now." She opened the car door so she could demonstrate.

Maggie lay stretched out in the back, red faced, panting, and sweaty.

"Now do you see?" Vera put her hands on her hips. "Am I vindicated?"

He frowned. "We'll have to talk about that later. It's better to get to the hospital in one piece, and the way you were driving, I'm not so sure about that."

"The way I was driving? What are you trying to say? Listen, I know how to handle a car. I was doing fine." She pointed her index finger in his direction for emphasis.

"Seriously? Because what I saw—"

Maggie interrupted with a blood curdling scream.

"It's too late. The baby's coming!"

Chapter 8

This couldn't be happening. His best friend's wife was about to give birth in the back of a car, and Vera wanted to argue about her racing skills.

Maggie screamed.

Vera didn't move. "What do we do?"

He'd wasted time arguing with her. There were so many things to do at once: radio dispatch for help, place flares on the road for safety, find some way to keep the baby warm, get blankets or towels, and deliver the baby.

Deliver the baby!

How was he supposed to do that? He'd had the same amount of CPR training as every other officer on the force, but he prayed he wouldn't need it. As for delivering babies, there was nothing in the manual about that.

He calculated how Vera could best help him. Panic was etched on every angle of her face in a way he'd never seen before. He had to calm her down, because he desperately needed her. He grasped her shoulders and tried to get her wild gaze to focus on his own.

"Here are my keys. In the trunk of my cruiser, I have a thermo blanket and a first aid kit. Bring that back to me and anything else you think we can use."

No time for the road flares. His cruiser with flashing lights behind Vera's car should be enough of a warning to any passing motorists.

He worried about the cold—approximately thirty degrees and definitely not the ideal kind of temperature for a newborn. They'd have to get the baby warm immediately.

He radioed dispatch for help and explained the situation. They'd send the paramedics and an ambulance. Unfortunately, unless they traveled at Mach 5 they were going to be too late.

He crouched outside the back door, halfway in. Maggie was stretched out on the small backseat sobbing.

"This is not happening. Not here. Not now." Maggie shook her head.

"Look at me, Maggie." He took her hand in his.

"You can do this."

They were out of time.

Ryan sent up a prayer. God was with them in this little car on the side of the road. He was always with them. Like He was with Ryan every time he went down the slopes, heart in his throat. And He would get them through this.

Vera arrived with the first aid kit, the thermo blanket, a towel he kept in the back for trips to the gym, a flashlight, a gallon of drinking water, and a granola bar.

"Are you hungry?" He took the first aid kit, thermo blanket, and towel and let her hold the rest for now.

She stared at the granola bar. "I grabbed everything."

"I need you to turn the car heater up as high as it will go. We need to keep it as warm in here as we can for the baby."

He took the water and poured some over his hands.

"What else can I do?" Vera got back in the car and bent over the front seat to reach for Maggie's hand.

"Pray for my baby," Maggie begged between moans.

"I will," Vera whispered.

Ryan exchanged looks with Vera. He hoped she would pray for him, too. Right now, he needed it.

"Dispatch, can you patch me through to the paramedics? Walk me through this?" He controlled his voice to what he hoped would be a soothing tone. No need to let Maggie know he had no clue what he was doing. He opened up the first aid kit and found a pair of plastic gloves.

"Hey, Ryan. It's Tagg Redfield with County. I'm going to walk you through. First check for the baby's head."

Ryan held his breath when he saw the baby's head clearly visible and continued to listen to Tagg's instructions.

"I want you to support the neck when the head comes out, and it may be any second now. Nature is pretty much going to take its course. When the baby comes out, wrap it in something warm. We're ETA four minutes."

"Did you hear that?" Ryan encouraged Maggie. Maggie shook her head. "I have to push!"

Vera brushed Maggie's hair aside. "It's OK. We're here. Your baby is going to be fine."

By the second push, the head was all the way out.

With the towel, Ryan supported its neck. "You're doing great," he assured Maggie.

Maggie moaned and pushed again, and the baby's shoulders and torso slipped out into Ryan's waiting hands, a milky white substance covering its body. He wiped the baby off with the towel.

Vera handed him the thermo blanket.

He wrapped it around the newborn, and then lifted him into Maggie's arms.

"Thank You, God. It's my baby boy. He's OK." Maggie cried.

The infant let out a loud squeal a second after being born. That had to be a good thing.

Relief flooded through Ryan. "I'll be right back." Ryan stepped away and shut the door to keep the heat inside.

"Ryan? How's everything?" Tagg asked over the radio.

"The baby's out. What's next?" He paced back and forth as adrenaline continued to surge through him.

"The placenta, for one."

"The what?" What else would the Lord have him learn tonight in this trial by fire?

Tagg laughed. "Don't worry, chief, I'll take care of it. ETA two minutes."

"Thanks. See that you do that." Placenta or not, Ryan could run a marathon right now. He could do anything. He'd brought a life into the world. *We did it. Thank You, Lord.*

THE PARAMEDICS ARRIVED. Vera relaxed.

The baby appeared small, though he sounded healthy enough, but a premature baby born in a hospital needed immediate care. This child, born before its time, wasn't receiving that care.

Vera lowered her head to collect her thoughts. She'd experienced a talk with God for the first time in years. In that car with Maggie's pain and the memories it stirred up, she'd almost lost hope. In the midst of it, she'd closed her eyes and prayed to the God of her youth. And He'd come through for all of them.

The medics said the baby would have to be placed in an incubator immediately. The men put mother and baby into the ambulance for the drive to the hospital.

Vera stood with Ryan in the middle of the road as the paramedics drove away carrying its precious cargo. She couldn't take her gaze off Ryan.

He shook his head and smiled. "What are you looking at?"

Without a second thought, she walked to him, wrapped her arms around his broad shoulders and held him tight. She brushed up against his cheek, kissed him softly on the lips, and then pulled away before he could kiss her back.

"Wow. I should deliver a baby more often." His brown eyes held hers. "Do you want to leave your car and follow them in the cruiser? I can put the sirens on." Thank the Lord he realized she didn't want to go home without making sure Maggie and the baby were pronounced healthy.

"Cruiser. Sirens."

"OK. Get in." Ryan opened the passenger door and then got in on his own side.

"Thank you for doing what you did back there. If it had been only me, I don't know what would have happened."

He put on his seatbelt. "You would have done it if you had to."

"No, I don't think so. I froze back there. I'm sorry I wasn't more help to you."

"Are you kidding? I couldn't have done it without you."

"What did I do? Bring you a granola bar?" She laughed.

"You brought everything you found in my trunk, which was helpful." He grinned and bit his lower lip.

"I was so scared, but you seemed calm. How did you find the courage and the peace?"

"I can't say that some of my training didn't help. We're taught not to panic since it doesn't help anything. But I wasn't alone. None of us were. God was with me and I prayed."

"For the first time in a long time, I did, too." The moments of intense prayer for the baby made every cell in her body tingle.

"Jack. One of us should call him," Ryan said.

He'd missed the birth of his first child. "He'll be so disappointed."

"He will be, but knowing Jack his first concern will be for their health and safety."

"The baby looked so small. I'm a little worried about that." Painful memories flooded back. She couldn't stop thinking of what Maggie would do if— no, she couldn't even let the thought enter her mind.

He took her hand in his and her heart skipped a beat. "He'll be fine. Did you hear the set of lungs he has on him?"

They arrived just behind the ambulance.

"They'll take them up to the labor and delivery floor. We can meet them up there." Ryan parked the cruiser and glanced at his watch. "I'll call Lonnie and see if he can come in early since I'm still on duty. I'll meet you inside."

Inside the well-lit and warm hospital, Vera asked for the way up to the L&D floor. Panic simmered and rose to the surface despite her best attempts to squash it. She sat in the waiting room.

Maggie was brought up via the elevator and came out the doors on a stretcher, her baby nowhere to be seen.

Vera's stomach dropped.

"Maggie!" she called out as the stretcher passed by. She followed it.

"Visiting hours are over now. Family only." A nurse stopped her.

"Vera, the baby's in intensive care," Maggie said and burst into tears.

"He's getting warm," a paramedic assured Maggie.

"I want my husband." Maggie sobbed.

"Excuse me." Vera tried to get past the hefty looking nurse. If she had to, she would push, but she hoped it wouldn't come to that. She fixed the woman with her best glare. "You should get out of my way."

"Ma'am—" The nurse began.

"She needs me," Vera interrupted. Ryan appeared behind her. "Hi, Sally."

"Hey, Ryan. Are you on duty?"

"Just got off. Hey, the patient's husband is out of town, and we're all good friends. She delivered in the car with Vera's help, and she's pretty scared." He indicated Vera to the nurse. "The baby's premature."

The nurse's lips formed a thin line. "Let me see what I can do." She walked away with a sidelong and somewhat disapproving glance in Vera's direction.

Vera folded her arms and sat down. "I am getting in there one way or another."

Ryan sat next to her. "I don't doubt it."

She glanced in his direction. He smiled.

The look unsettled her, and she squirmed.

"I called Jack, and they're trying to get a flight out tonight. He won't be here 'til tomorrow morning at the earliest."

"Is he upset?"

"He wanted to know if they were OK."

"Ryan, the baby wasn't with Maggie. Do you think he's all right?"

"They had to warm him up, remember?"

She prayed that was all there was to it, but he was so tiny. So helpless.

The silence stretched between them.

The day had been a long one. She'd love to go home and climb into—oh, no. She bounded to her feet.

"Stin!"

Ryan stood. "What's wrong?"

"She's been alone all day since I was at the baby shower. I want to stay with Maggie, but I need to feed Stin and let her out." She'd been so busy it had slipped her mind.

Poor Stin was probably waiting at the door by now. With her bowl.

"That's OK, I'll go. Give me your keys, and tell me where the food is." He looked so sincere. This man had to be some kind of cosmic joke.

"But Stin doesn't really like men." That was silly. Stin liked food enough that she might overlook a man feeding her.

"I don't mind if she doesn't." Ryan stared with an intensity that shook her.

"Um, sure. Maybe if you speak softly." It wasn't like she had much choice in the matter. Stin would have to get over herself. Vera handed over the house keys and explained where he could find the dog food.

"And about your car—I took care of that, too."

She had almost forgotten about her abandoned car. "How did you do that?"

"I called in a favor." He grinned. "And obviously it will need to be cleaned, too. I know someone who does great work."

She thanked God for Ryan. Even when she didn't seem to be able to string two thoughts together, his mind fired on all cylinders. She was about to kiss him again, but the nurse returned.

"All right, she's settled in. You can see her now."

When they reached Maggie's room, they found the new mother a bit calmer than before.

Vera didn't see a crib anywhere. She hugged Maggie, and then moved aside so that Ryan could do the same.

"My heroes." Instead of exhaustion, Maggie's eyes were as alert as if she'd had a cup of espresso.

"Where's the baby?" Vera asked.

"He's still getting warm," Maggie said.

"Is he OK?" Vera managed to squeak out.

"Yes, he's fine. I'm sorry if I scared you." Maggie smiled. "I guess I was kind of out of it for a little bit."

"No one blames you," Ryan said.

"How do you know he's going to be OK if you haven't seen him?" Guilt pressed the issue.

Babies needed time to grow in the womb. Vera remembered facts she hadn't thought about in years but didn't want to dwell on them now.

"She said he's fine." Ryan touched her elbow and gave it a slight squeeze.

They were both being optimistic, which she could appreciate, but probably neither one of them had any experience with premature babies. Yet there was a peace about both of them.

She wished she could have some of it right now.

"They put him in a warmer to get his temperature up." Maggie had a soft smile on her face. "I held him for a few minutes. Now they're putting him through some tests. The nurse tells me he's already been weighed, and he's five pounds and seven ounces. Imagine how big he would have been full term."

"A linebacker." Ryan grinned. "I got a hold of Jack. He and Lexi are doing their best to get a flight out tonight. You may not be able to reach him now if he's in the air."

"That explains why he didn't answer his phone. I just tried calling him."

Ryan stepped back. "I need to run some errands. I think you should be able to stay here, Vera, if you want."

"Yes, please stay. I want you to see my baby again.

This time all cleaned up," Maggie said.

"Of course I will. Until Jack gets here," she said, despite the antiseptic smells of the hospital and the too-white walls that begged her to flee.

Ryan had done the hard part.

Now it was time for Vera to be the best friend.

Ryan walked out the door, and Vera sat in the chair next to Maggie.

"I don't need you to stay here all night. You need to go home and sleep in a bed. These chairs are for tired husbands and mine isn't here," Maggie said.

"You're talking to someone who used to travel a lot. I've slept in my share of airports waiting for delayed flights." Vera touched Maggie's hand. "I'm staying."

"You poor thing. Your hand is shaking. I'm sorry I scared you," Maggie said. "This didn't exactly go according to plan."

"No it didn't."

Births didn't always go according to expectations.

Nor did a young woman's dreams.

"I'm thanking God that you were with me. I'd probably been in labor most of the baby shower, but I tried to ignore it. Bad idea." No wonder she'd looked so uncomfortable.

"Yeah, don't you do that again. Ever." Vera smiled. "I'm thankful, too, for Ryan. I panicked. But I almost got you to the hospital on time. Maybe if Ryan hadn't pulled me over."

Maggie laughed. "Ryan is something else, isn't he?

I'll never be able to thank him enough."

Vera nodded. He was something all right.

Something that took her breath away.

"I was so mad at him at the baby shower this afternoon and now I can't even muster it back up."

"You were? Why?"

Vera frowned. "He put me on the list for the foundation, and today, at the shower, they called me. We've talked about this for weeks, and he knows my feelings about it. I told him that I didn't want to do that, and he ignored me."

"But when we had lunch together, you told me you'd find out more about it."

"That was before I heard about the race. Both Ryan and I are in this tournament. If neither of us wins and, of course, there's a good chance I won't, maybe then."

"Ryan's in the tournament, too?"

"He offered to increase my odds of winning. If he wins he'll give me the purse."

"He will?" Maggie's eyes widened. "That's amazing."

"I agree."

"I always suspected Ryan had a secret crush on you. Now I'm convinced."

"Crush? On me and every other eligible woman in town."

Surely, Maggie hadn't forgotten that he'd even asked her out before she'd met Jack.

"No, it's different with you. I think it always was. Tell me, how many other women has he offered to win tournaments for? None that I'm aware of." She crossed her arms.

Vera wasn't going there. Not to a place where she could see herself with a man like Ryan. A place where she didn't belong. "Me either."

"And what if neither of you win? If you wait too long to ask for the foundation's help, it may be too late. There are so many who need help and only so much money to go around," Maggie said.

"All the more reason to leave it to someone more deserving."

Maggie shut her eyes and bit her lower lip. "OK. But, Vera, please don't be mad at Ryan. I was the one who called the foundation."

Chapter 9

Ryan pulled up to Vera's house. Her car was parked in the driveway as expected. He'd thank his new friend, Bible study partner, and towing business owner, Alan, later.

Stin ran from the front door when she saw him enter, but as soon as he got out the dog food she emerged tentatively from Vera's bedroom and followed him into the kitchen. He placed her bowl on the floor and watched as she studied it, sniffed it, then eyed him again.

"Where's the trust?"

With a wag of her tail, she began to eat.

"Smart girl."

Being alone in Vera's home seemed a bit like intruding on her privacy.

But something memorable had happened to both of them tonight. He couldn't deny it. Vera had locked eyes with him, an unspoken message between them. He only wished he had a clue about her thoughts.

More amazing, Vera had prayed. He was sure of it. He'd glanced at her before the baby was born and caught a glimpse of her eyes closed peacefully as though in a private moment.

After everything she'd told him about her past with her ex-husband, it made sense that Vera had become estranged from the church. In her position, he might have done the same. But in his case, neither one of his parents had ever taken him to church. His best friend had led him in the right direction. He wished he could do the same for Vera.

A car door slammed outside and Ryan glanced out the window.

Vera's ex marched to the front door. *This guy doesn't know when to quit.*

But it was good he came now, while Ryan was here. Vera might have been vulnerable alone in the house. Stin was no guard dog. Ryan waited a few seconds after

Kevin rang the doorbell before opening the door.

Stin followed him to the door, but took one look at the man standing on the threshold and scurried back into Vera's bedroom.

"Yeah, I don't blame you," Ryan muttered under his breath. "Can I help you?" He stared at Kevin.

If Kevin was surprised to see Ryan at the door, it hardly registered in his empty eyes. "I'd like to see Vera."

"Sorry. She's not here."

Kevin looked toward the driveway. "Her car is here."

"Yes it is."

Kevin cocked his head to the side. "When will she be back?"

"I'm not sure. Maybe I can help you." Kevin smiled widely. "I doubt that."

"Why not try?"

"I see what's happening here."

"Do you?" He somehow doubted that.

"Has Vera hired you as security? Is she that paranoid?"

Of course, he would think that. No way would he consider a small-town deputy sheriff to be any kind of competition for him. "More to the point, does she have reason to be?"

"Absolutely not. But spending money to hire security when she's in the mess she's in, well that's going overboard." Kevin locked a hostile gaze with Ryan.

"If you say so." Ryan wasn't going to correct him.

Let him think he was security. In a way he was.

"But it must be an easy gig for you—security for a beautiful woman, a former fashion model. Probably don't see women like her around here much."

Ryan stared without speaking.

"No, I can't blame you. Vera has always spent more than she has. Why should it stop now?"

"How's that again?" That caught his attention. He'd always seen Vera as someone with expensive taste, but he'd assumed she could afford it and that this financial problem was unusual.

"She's high maintenance. While we were married, I spent most of my money buying her whatever she wanted trying to keep her happy."

"What is it you want? Why are you here?" Ryan changed the subject.

Kevin took a step back. Good. Ryan had rattled him.

"Simple. I want to help."

"You don't want to help. What you want is to take away the one thing Vera has left. The café is not for sale." He took a step toward Kevin.

"And on whose authority do you speak?" Kevin frowned.

"On my friend's authority. She's not selling."

"Now she's a friend. If Vera gets desperate enough, she'll sell the café."

"She'll never be that desperate."

"That's what you think."

"It's what I know."

"Don't tell me you've encouraged this crazy half- baked idea of winning that ski tournament?"

Ryan ignored that remark and glanced at the Rolls.

"I've been meaning to tell you. A red curb means no parking. I've seen your car parked around town and never in the right place."

"Did you ever stop to think you need more parking spaces in this two bit town?"

"Next time I see it in a red zone, I'm having it towed. I'll tell Vera you came by." He shut the door.

Stin peered out from the bedroom to assess whether it was safe to come out again. *Pretty smart dog.*

Ryan turned off the lights and locked the door.

Kevin had painted a picture of a selfish and materialistic woman, one who didn't sound at all like the woman he'd come to know.

Ryan had made his own mistakes in the past and given far too much attention to what money could buy. He'd made a good living with skiing and had taken some chances.

After the accident, he'd decided to obtain a degree in criminology as he'd always dreamed. Then he'd entered the police academy. Sure, there was no real money in his profession, but the satisfaction he got every day from making a difference was priceless.

Could Vera ever be happy as the wife of

a public servant? He shook his head. What did that matter?

They were just good friends. Even if his heart had other ideas.

VERA STARED. Maggie had put Vera's name on the list without her consent. Good thing she hadn't torn into Ryan with her accusations. She opened her mouth to speak.

A nurse wheeled the baby in the room.

"Here he is. All warmed up and ready for Mom," the nurse said.

"Do you want to hold him, Vera?" Maggie asked.

Before Vera could decline, the nurse picked him up from the plastic crib and placed him in her shaking arms.

She backed up to the chair and sat down, afraid her trembling legs might not hold her up. The powdery, clean smell of newborn baby caused her to inhale deeply.

His tiny fists were raised up next to his face like a little boxer. It hardly seemed possible, but he would be fine.

She pushed back tears. "Have you picked out a name yet? I can't keep calling him the baby."

"It was to be John Vincent, after Jack's grandfather. But now I will have to see how I can work Ryan and Vera into his name." Maggie laughed.

The baby's cheeks were a healthy pink. Bundled up he didn't look as small as Vera remembered. *Thank you, God. He's going to live.* "Don't be silly. John. What a beautiful name. Simple, but strong."

This baby was a fighter. And he had a great story to tell his own children someday.

"I'm sorry. I shouldn't have put your name on the foundation list. But when Ryan told me about the tournament, I panicked." Maggie winced.

"I would have told you, but I didn't want you to worry." Vera touched John's impossibly soft cheek.

"You know me too well. It sounds too dangerous."

"I don't want you to worry about me. You have enough on your plate."

"I'm never too busy for you." Vera wanted to believe that.

But they lived in different worlds since Maggie married Jack. Maggie was no longer a single mother parenting her troubled teenaged daughter. Back then, Vera and

Maggie were thick as thieves. But then Jack had entered the picture, and it made sense that there was less time for their friendship.

"Don't worry. I'm a pretty decent skier. And Ryan has been training with me." Interesting that she could breathe evenly with John in her arms. She sat still, afraid the smallest movement might injure him.

Maggie leaned forward. "You've been spending a lot of time with Ryan, haven't you?"

Vera flushed, and not because of the warmth in the room, or the fact that the baby lay in her arms. "It's possible that Ryan has changed."

"I tried to tell you that. And I think you two would be perfect together."

"You do?" This didn't surprise her.

Maggie wouldn't be happy until the whole world was filled with unicorns and rainbows.

"It always seemed that you were two of a kind. Male and female versions of the same person. You both like to have a good time, and neither one of you ever wanted to settle down. Not to mention that you're both the most stubborn people I've ever met."

"Hmmm. Maybe you have a point."

"Why didn't you ever go out with him? I wondered about that, too."

That one was harder to explain. Maybe on some deeper level she'd sensed that being with Ryan would be complicated. "You can wonder all you want."

The baby began to squirm in Vera's arms and his face turned frightening shades of red. Unnerved, Vera handed him back to Maggie. Exhaustion seeped into Vera as the night's events took their toll. Combined with the punishing workouts and days on the slopes, Vera felt every one of her thirty-two years.

The nurse came in and handed Vera an extra pillow and a blanket. "You can stay if you like. I won't say anything."

Vera marveled at the influence Ryan had on rigid female nurses. She settled in to the stiff hospital chair. Her eyelids drooped.

Maggie seemed to be sailing on a considerable second wind. "Take a nap," Maggie said.

"Shouldn't you be the tired one?" Vera yawned and stretched.

"No, I've got that new-mother surge of energy and adrenaline. I could stay up all night. In fact, maybe I will."

"I wouldn't advise it." The nurse took the baby and placed him in the rolling crib. "You should take advantage of the nursery while you can."

"No. I want him to stay with me." Maggie placed her hand on the crib and stopped its movement.

"Suit yourself, but call if you need anything." The nurse walked out of the room.

Vera had seen her sister, Amy, act the same way with her babies. Not for the first time, Vera wondered what kind of mother she might have been if she'd had the chance. As she drifted off to sleep, she prayed someday she'd have the privilege of holding her own baby.

For the first time in years, she dreamt of her baby girl again. Her own little secret, piercing pain. She never talked about her anymore, as though she'd never existed. At one time, that had been more painful, but now, well some women were just not meant to be mothers.

Vera awoke with tears in her eyes. Conscious of whispering sounds, she wiped her eyes and blinked at the scene before her.

Jack lay in the bed next to Maggie and held his baby son.

Lexi stood on the other side of Maggie.

Vera had apparently slept for hours, the only awareness of the length of time being the severity of the crick in her neck.

"Aunt Vera, isn't he beautiful?" Lexi squealed.

"You're awake," Maggie said.

"Hmm." Vera massaged her neck. This kind of knot might never come out.

"Hey, thanks for your help, V." The bags under Jack's eyes and the days' worth of beard growth couldn't conceal the joy in his eyes.

"I didn't do anything. Ryan was the hero. I was the crazy driver."

"I heard you were speeding again." Jack frowned.

"In my defense, I almost got her to the hospital in time."

"I can't blame you. I might have done the same," Jack said.

"Well thanks for that, Sheriff." Vera stood and stretched.

Ryan walked in the room holding a bouquet of flowers.

Lexi hugged him.

After greetings and hugs all around, Jack handed his son to Ryan. "You need to hold him. He probably looks a lot better than the first time you did."

Ryan held the baby close, like fear was not part of the equation and as though he'd been doing it his whole life.

"What do you think, Vera? Want to hold him?" Ryan met her gaze.

"That's OK, I held him last night." She had to get out of here.

Jack and Lexi were back, and Maggie wouldn't be alone now.

Vera had a business to run, and a tournament to win. "I need to get going. I couldn't reach Annie last night so I don't know if she got my message to open up this morning. For all I know there's a line of people waiting."

"I drove by this morning, and she must have gotten your message." Ryan gave the baby back to Maggie.

"Good. Well, I have to get to the gym. My trainer is a real stickler," Vera teased.

"That he is. I can give you a ride," Ryan said.

"You and the gym? Why?" Lexi cocked her head to the side.

"I'll tell you later," Maggie said.

Jack moved toward the door as Vera and

Ryan were leaving. "I'll be right back, baby," Jack said to Maggie.

Vera should have seen it coming. In the hallway, she faced both Ryan and Jack, like two handsome matching bookends.

"What's this about a ski tournament?" Jack asked.

"I think you already know." Vera narrowed her eyes.

"It's not a good idea," Jack said.

"Save it. Ryan has already given it his best." Vera folded her arms.

Ryan nodded. "And she won't listen."

"I won't argue. I know what it's like when a woman makes up her mind," Jack said.

"Smart man." Vera nodded.

"Just be careful. There are a lot of people who care about you and don't want to see you hurt." Jack touched her shoulder.

The kindness in his eyes lowered her defenses.

"Don't worry. I will."

"And I'll make sure of it." Ryan met her gaze.

•   •   •

RYAN OPENED the passenger door of the cruiser, and Vera eased into the front seat.

"It was getting a little too sweet in there for me," she said.

"I used to feel that way until I realized the problem was jealousy." No reason to mince words. He wanted exactly what Jack and Maggie had—a family. No matter how far he'd tried to run from that fact it had still caught up with him.

Vera gazed at him with narrowed eyes. "You jealous? Why?"

"Who wouldn't want what they have? You can practically feel the love pouring out into the hallways." He pulled out of the hospital parking lot.

"Babies scare me. So much can go wrong." She slid down in her seat.

"He's going to be OK."

Vera's fears seemed excessive, but the unexpected birth had shocked him, too. He'd been distressed and in completely uncharted territory, but Vera seemed shaken to the core. He'd seen it in her wild gaze, unfocused for the first time. Flying down treacherous mountains trails didn't faze her, but a newborn knocked her off course? It didn't make sense.

"I hope so. But it's still so much to risk."

"I don't think so. Love is worth it. I know I want a family someday. Don't you?" He'd come full circle in that regard. Running from responsibility was another part of his past. Holding Jack's baby today had affirmed his feelings. One day, God willing, he'd be a father, too.

"No. Some people are not meant to be parents."

The certainty in her voice rattled him. Next subject. "I've been meaning to ask if you've had any more thoughts about the foundation. It's not too late to get their help."

"They called me. Maggie put me on the list."

"She did? That's great."

"No, it's not. Someone else should get that assistance. Maybe one of the church members."

"But why not you? We're not only helping people who attend church. That's not the point. I'm proud that we're doing something in the community to help everyone who needs it." He gripped the steering wheel tighter.

"I'd rather not."

He'd had enough of her vague excuses. As they turned on Main Street, he pulled the truck over in front of Katie's bookstore. Time to get to the bottom of this.

"Why are we stopping here?" Vera shifted in her seat.

He shut off the car and turned in his seat to face her. "You have to tell me now. Why not you? What makes you so undeserving?"

Vera folded her arms and looked out the window.

"I'm not doing this now."

"C'mon, did you rob a bank or something I'm not aware of? This might be a good time to confess." He grinned, but the feeble attempt at humor apparently did not sit well with Vera.

She glared at him. "I'm not a good person. OK?"

"Neither am I, darlin'."

"Please don't tell me that. You help everybody.

You're a hero to everyone you meet."

"I'm trying. A work in progress. If you don't think I struggle, you're wrong. I'm human, too."

"You look human." She bit her lip.

"Unless you did cheat as Kevin accused, you have no reason to feel guilty about anything. No reason not to accept help." Now it was out in the open.

"Is that what you think?" Vera glared at him, a fire in her eyes.

"Not at all. But tell me. Do you blame yourself in some way? Because you're acting like you do."

"Listen to me, Colton. I never broke my vows. Even though everyone thought I did. And, yeah, maybe I should have tried harder to make the marriage work. But I did everything I could. It takes two people to save a marriage. "

"You're right. Look at me," he said, waiting until her gaze met his. "I'm not judging you."

"Maybe not you, but if I take money from the foundation, I can't help but think that someday I'll do something wrong. And they'll turn on me. I'm not perfect and I won't ever be."

In that moment, he had to tell her the truth. He took her hand. "I want to tell you about my accident."

"Now?"

"You wanted to know. I don't talk about

it because the whole thing was my fault. Breaking my back. Six months of traction. My fault."

"You broke your back? How was that your fault?"

"Because I was drunk." Not even the worst thing he'd ever done, but it was now out in the open.

Her blue eyes widened, but he didn't see any judgment in them. "You were?"

"The night before, I'd been out late drinking and having fun 'til the morning hours. The alcohol was still in my system when I had to race the next morning. Of course, there was no way I was going to bow out. That would have looked bad. And I paid for my pride."

"Is that why you haven't skied in years?"

"Maybe. I used to relive the accident every time I'd get up on a pair of skis."

"Used to? Ryan, you entered the tournament even though the last time you skied you broke your back?" Tears filled Vera's eyes.

The last thing he'd intended was to make her cry.

"I had to get back out there, eventually.

And you know what? I've enjoyed it." After the first few days of heart palpitations.

Vera didn't say anything.

Maybe he'd been successful in convincing her he was no angel. She'd probably want another trainer.

She unbuckled her seatbelt and moved to him, embracing him without any words. Her head rested on his shoulder while he opened his arms and pulled her near, closing his eyes.

"Do you still think I'm a good person?" he whispered in her ear.

"Yes. I do."

They held each other until a few pedestrians stared into the truck.

He didn't want to let go. He'd given her the biggest part of his heart.

Yet she hadn't told him why she couldn't accept the foundation's help.

But Vera had broken down the last defenses of his heart.

Chapter 10

The first qualifying race was only one day away. Vera flew down the slope. The sharp hiss of her skis was a comfort. Thanks to Ryan's help, her speed had improved due to the new form and control she had adopted.

If only she could exert the same discipline over her emotions. She'd nearly lost her determination to keep that tight control when Ryan's brown eyes had stared into hers. There was nothing but warmth and love and none of the fear she expected to see given the knowledge of his accident.

The truth had slammed into her like a freight train. Ryan would not only give her the purse if he won. He had also faced great fear. To see him push off the hill, one would never know there had been an accident.

Still, doubts occupied her mind day and night. No one had ever sacrificed so much for her. The possibility still existed that Ryan was feeding her a line, and if he won, he'd walk away with the money. He owed her absolutely nothing. She would do well to remember that.

She couldn't share what she'd done. Maybe someday she'd have the courage to tell him. For now her bravery would have to be limited to the race, which she had a chance of winning. *Right.*

Ryan sidled up beside her at the end of the run.

"Great job. You've improved in every way. Want to go again?"

"You should practice your own runs. I don't want to take time away from you."

"I'll do that later."

For the last few weeks, he'd spent all of his free time with her. He was nothing like the outrageous flirt she remembered and she wondered how anyone could change so completely. "One more for me and that's it. I need to call it a day." She walked to the ski lift with Ryan.

Kyle and his entourage approached. The man always had women surrounding him. Even the ones who weren't skiing would walk with him to the lift just to stand there and wave.

"You still here?" Kyle grinned at Vera.

"I can't make it too easy for you, can I?"

"That's the spirit." Kyle walked away chuckling.

"Was it that way for you, too? Always people hanging around?" Especially women, she wanted to add, but reconsidered.

Ryan shrugged. "Everybody loves a winner."

"So the answer is yes?"

"The answer is, when I won."

She looked for a hint of bitterness in his gaze, but there was nothing but heart in those deep brown eyes.

At the top of the hill, she and Ryan lined up for their last freestyle run of the day. She'd finally risen to his level and they often raced each other down the hill. Every one of her muscles ached and screamed in protest, but one more run couldn't hurt. Then she'd go home and lie in a hot steamy bath and relax. She started off slightly ahead of Ryan.

He passed her on the second leg. Eyes on

him, she made him a target. She'd pass him. That would prove to him that she was ready for this, as ready as she'd ever be. Maybe then, she'd get him to drop out of the race. After all, she couldn't face it if he won and walked away with the money. Or worse, if he was injured again.

Crouching, she put all her speed into it, forming her skis into two parallel lines. One minute into her new found lift, her right leg lost control as though the quivering muscles could no longer hold her up.

Red hot searing pain created a burning agony beyond words. Vera opened her mouth to scream, but the air was pushed from her lungs as she hit the ground and rolled in drifts of white powder. The pain overcame her as she fell into darkness.

AMAZING how skiing for the right reasons had taken every last vestige of fear away. God had come through for him with the additional gift he'd never imagined he could receive. Renewed appreciation for the sport as it had been once, before it had taken over his life.

Not only that. He'd become aware that

he had nothing left to prove to Vera or anyone else. If she couldn't see that he'd changed, it didn't matter. The Lord knew how his heart had changed.

He reached the bottom of the hill expecting to see Vera right behind him.

She'd gained control of her speed and closed another gap between her and the other skilled skiers.

He lifted his gaze.

A small crowd gathered around a downed skier. He recognized the pink jacket and blonde hair spilling out the side of the helmet. *No.*

He dropped his poles and unhooked from his skis so that he could race back up the hill, never an easy thing in snow. Adrenaline pumping, he fixed his gaze on Vera, who lay helpless on the ground. He fought against the rising sense of panic. He needed to trust God.

Vera was too quiet in the snow, eyes closed in an unnaturally peaceful look for someone who enjoyed verbally sparring with him every day. He knelt beside her and gently removed her helmet, grateful not to see any blood.

"Vera, can you hear me?" Ryan shouted.

Vera's eyes fluttered opened. She moaned as she sat up and reached for her ankle.

He was afraid of that. "You must have twisted it coming down."

Vera's eyes rolled in the back and she mouthed words with no sound.

He feared she'd broken her foot or ankle, or had torn a ligament. Maybe he shouldn't have pushed her so hard for one last run. All those workouts in the gym added to the days on the slope had perhaps pushed her body too far. He may have finally circumvented her attempt to win the race, but not in the way he'd imagined.

Several more concerned skiers gathered around them. He handed one of the skiers her poles, and then cautiously removed her skis.

He lifted her and carried her off the trail. "Can you call up a snowmobile?" he asked a fellow skier.

Vera had fallen several hundred feet from the bottom of the mountain, and he wouldn't be able to carry her down on his own.

Vera opened her eyes.

"How do you feel?" A dumb question,

but her ability to answer would tell him a great deal.

She sobbed against him.

The crying wrenched his heart. She would miss the first qualifying race, effectively disqualifying her from going any further. She'd proved she had courage, but this was the end of the line. The injury looked serious enough that he prayed it wouldn't sideline her from skiing permanently.

He removed her boot carefully even as she slapped his hand away in a classic effort to protect herself from the pain. "I'm not going to hurt you, darlin'," he soothed.

The ankle had already swollen.

He gently placed her foot in the snow and carefully created a pile around her ankle to ice it.

The snowmobile arrived within minutes.

He placed her in the back. He would get their equipment later. He didn't want to leave her side until he had her with adequate medical personnel.

The first-aid station at Dodge Ridge would not be equipped for this type of emergency.

As a first responder, he knew that they normally referred everyone to the nearby hospital. The temporary medical staff and their equipment would probably arrive tomorrow in time for the tournament.

The health clerk in the first-aid office took one look at Vera's ankle and pronounced it broken. "You'll need to get her to the hospital. Only an X-ray can tell for certain."

"No." Vera moaned. "I want to go home." The health clerk gave Ryan a puzzled look.

"She's not thinking straight. We need to get her warm. Does she look pale to you?"

"We could call an ambulance. I wish there was more we could do." The clerk applied an ice pack for the swelling, gave Vera over-the-counter pain medication, and placed the ankle in a temporary restraint.

"I'll drive her to the hospital." There wasn't any other option.

Vera found her voice. "You will not."

He couldn't stand one more minute of her bullheaded ways. "We don't have a choice." He took her face in his hands and forced her dazed blue eyes to meet his own.

Against her heated implorations to put her down, Ryan carried Vera from the first aid station to his truck.

"Put me down!" Vera shouted.

"Stop acting like an idiot."

He carried her by a group of kids lined up with their snowboards at the entrance and placed her in the back seat.

A kid Ryan recognized from church looked at him with wide eyes. "Is she under arrest, Mr. Colton?"

Sometimes, he had to admit, the idea had its appeal. Ryan started to say no, but then shook his head. "I don't know, kid. Maybe."

From the backseat Vera tried to slap his head, but he dodged her in time.

"Someone else can take me to the hospital. You need to get back to the slopes."

"If you don't quit, I'll ask the doctor to X-ray your head, too. I'm taking you. That's it." He started the drive to the hospital they'd left only a few hours ago.

"I'm counting on you now more than ever. You're my only shot at winning."

Great. No pressure. He didn't think he had much of a shot against Kyle, even though the local paper had ranked his odds as better than he believed them to be. Instead he worried he'd freeze up on race day.

He hadn't so far, but winning hadn't been on the line. Yet.

He'd mixed himself up in a crazy long shot for the sake of a woman who didn't have the good sense to let him take her to the hospital. Sometimes he wondered why he bothered at all.

Ryan pulled up to the hospital's emergency room entrance. Opening the back door, he found a frowning Vera.

"I can walk," she snapped.

"No way. You shouldn't put any weight on it." He ought to let her try. Maybe then, she'd believe him.

For once, she was leaning on him, but it was only out of necessity. She hopped alongside, keeping her injured foot off the floor.

By the time she was admitted and in a room in ER, her ankle had swollen to about twice its normal size.

He paced the room and asked for help several times before the physician finally appeared.

"Ski accident, eh? It is that time of the year." The physician examined her ankle and immediately ordered an X-ray. Then he called a nurse in to give Vera some pain medication.

An orderly appeared soon afterward and began to wheel Vera away. She glanced behind her. "Are you coming?" she asked.

He hadn't planned to, but this woman of mystery seemed to need him now. He walked beside the wheelchair as it rolled down the hallway, surprised when Vera reached out and grabbed his hand. Fear emanated from her and he held her hand until they were separated at the X-ray room.

Alone, he finally had a moment to think and bent his head in silent prayer for the woman who seemed to have a knack for driving him crazy.

In a way, the problem was resolved.

Vera, sidelined from the competition, would be safe now. Despite her broken ankle, he would consider that an answered prayer.

Now, all he'd have to do was qualify for the finals and win the tournament for her. Just that small thing. *Right.*

AFTER THE X-RAY, Vera was thankful to be back in the emergency room. Ryan hadn't left her side even though she'd done her best to get him to stay on the slopes. Now, she didn't want him to go anywhere. He'd brought her here to a hospital, her least favorite place in the world, and by golly, she didn't want him to leave her here without a friend.

And he was a good friend.

Unfortunately, she was beginning to care a little too much for this good friend and that troubled her. But soon the tournament would be over and they would go their separate ways. Hopefully, they'd still be friends after all she'd put the poor guy through.

She'd been a fool when she insisted on entering the contest, especially since Ryan had volunteered to take her place. Now all she had to show for her efforts was a possibly broken ankle, weeks of recuperation, and more bills to add to the pile. And quite likely, she would lose her home, anyway.

Ryan paced the room with long strides as they waited again for the doctor. He drew a hand through his close cropped hair and heaved repeated sighs followed by glares at the clock. Fourteen years ago, she'd been in a hospital a long way from home for a much more serious reason, and yet no one had made half the fuss over her that Ryan made now.

"How shorthanded can they be, for crying out loud? I've had faster service at the DMV," Ryan complained. "Are you doing OK?"

"It doesn't hurt anymore." The room seemed to spin a little, but in a good way.

He gazed in her eyes as though he'd pulled her over for being under the influence.

"It's the meds they gave you. Hope they don't make you loopy."

"I'm not loopy, snoopy." *Ryan.* How could she have missed the best man in town, right under her nose the entire time?

Ryan stared at her. "Great. They gave you way too much medication."

"Don't worry about me, buddy. I'm not driving." She shook her finger.

"You can say that again."

"Come here." He now stood by the door, way too far away. Her index finger beckoned him to her side.

He moved closer. His eyes narrowed. "What's up?"

She took his arms, pulled him even closer, and framed his face in her hands. "I want to kiss you."

"Vera…"

Their lips met for a glorious moment before he pulled away. "No, Vera. This isn't right. You're not yourself."

"I'm very much myself. Who else could I be?"

"That's it. I'm getting you some coffee. Be right back." He turned and marched out of the room.

While Ryan was gone, the doctor entered with the X-rays. He placed them in the viewer, hit the switch, and she observed the view of her ankle and its contrasting patches of darkness and light.

"You're a lucky lady."

"Thank you, Doctor. I agree." Now if only she could get Ryan to shut up and kiss her.

He frowned at her. "It's actually a hairline fracture. So the good news is you can wear a medic boot. The bad news is you can forget about skiing for a while." The doctor pointed at the small fracture.

"What about work? I own a café, and I have to get back to it."

The doctor scrunched up his nose, which made him look like a rabbit.

She pinched her arm to keep from laughing.

"You need to stay home for a couple of days and rest. Then you should be able to resume regular duties as long as you promise to take it easy on that foot. But you'll need to keep the boot on for several weeks to heal properly. I'll get the nurse to fit you, and then we can release you. And don't forget to follow up with your own doctor."

The bad news sobered her. She'd already spent too much time away from the café and couldn't possibly stay away any longer. Annie was racking up the overtime. Still more bills to pay.

Ryan appeared with her coffee. Things could be worse. His soulful brown eyes, dark hair, and even his beard stubble made her heart do a strange flip. *Oh yeah, I could be falling in love with my friend, a good man who deserves someone much better than me.*

He handed her the coffee. "This will sober you up.

I heard the good news. It's only a hairline fracture."

"You have a funny idea of what qualifies as good news." Vera stuck her tongue out at him.

"Hey, I'm only trying to look at the bright side. Amazing, since you acted like your foot had been cut off." He sat in the chair next to the exam table and smirked.

"You have no idea how much it hurt," she protested.

"I don't doubt it, darlin'."

She loved the sound of that word on his lips, as if it were meant only for her. "And by the way, I don't want you to compete tomorrow." As crazy as that sounded, she'd given it enough thought in the past few minutes. She didn't want him to win because she might have to find out that he'd never give her that purse. Their friendship would not survive.

And she couldn't be responsible for him. She couldn't stand the thought if he got hurt because of her. Her foolish plans had to stop now.

"That's the meds talking."

"No, Ryan. I mean it."

"What's this? I thought you didn't even want me to take time away to take you to the hospital. Now you don't want me to compete?" His brow furrowed.

"You don't have to anymore. It was a crazy idea, and I see that now."

"*Now* you see it? Did anyone ever tell you that you have lousy timing?" He didn't know the half of it. "I'll accept help from the foundation, if it's not too late. I'll call them right away. I'm already on the list." Thanks to Maggie.

"What changed your mind?" He narrowed his eyes.

"This." She looked at her foot. "You finally got through to me. Aren't you happy?"

"Sure, but apparently my timing also leaves something to be desired." He ran his thumb along the rim of his foam cup.

"You don't have to do this."

"Oh, yes, I do. I'm not a quitter. I started this thing. I intend to finish it. And besides, if I win the money, it's yours. If you don't want it, it can go to the foundation. Either way, it will help someone in need. Kyle has enough money. I probably should have thought of it the minute I heard about the purse. I don't know what my chances are, but I'm going to try. I'll get as far as I can, and hopefully, I'll win."

"I can't talk you out of this?" She didn't like the determined look on his face, the set jaw, the steely look in his warm brown eyes.

"Two can play the stubborn game. I'm pretty determined, too, when I want to be."

Maybe they truly were two of a kind, as Maggie had said.

"I don't want you to get hurt again. I've asked too much of you already."

"You didn't ask, remember?" His penetrating eyes melted her resolve. He brushed hair from her forehead with such tenderness that she wanted to cry.

Too bad she had not met him long ago, before she'd made the kind of foolish choices that would make it impossible to be with someone like Ryan.

"NOT EXACTLY STYLIN', are you?" Ryan grinned at the huge black boot on Vera's foot. For someone who always looked like she'd stepped out of the pages of a fashion magazine, whether she wore an apron or ski garb on the slopes, it had to be difficult.

"I'll accessorize somehow." Vera shrugged.

He'd brought his truck around to the front curb and opened the door for her as she rose from the wheelchair and tentatively stepped toward the car. He held the crutches they'd given her, worried she'd trip.

As soon as he got her home, he had to get back to the slopes and recover their equipment. Tomorrow, he would have to report to the slopes early for the first competitive run. If he advanced, and he thought he would, then he would be in Kyle's league.

The old competitive energy rose up unbidden. He hadn't fallen for Kyle's taunting, but when he possessed the desire to win for a good cause, every bit of spirit was there for him. Just like God had promised it would be.

Now he had to make sure to keep his own fears in check. And if Vera had the courage to do it, he could, too.

He scanned Vera's neighborhood to make certain that Kevin was not parked anywhere near her house again. Then he told her all about Kevin's unexpected visit.

"He thought I'd hired you for security?" Vera laughed.

"I'll just say I didn't dissuade him from thinking that."

"I hope you scared him off."

"I think maybe I did. Let's hope so." He opened the door for Vera and held out his hand. She accepted it without slapping it away. *Progress.* He helped her get inside the door to a waiting and jumping Stin, who promptly jumped on her boot.

"Ow. This is where obedience school would have come in handy. Down, Stin."

"Are you going to be all right?"

"Of course I am. I'm not an invalid."

Still, the way she gritted her teeth as she ambled forward led him to believe otherwise. She staggered along with slow and unsure steps.

He took her hand and led her to the couch. "Here, sit down."

Stin sniffed the boot and then jumped up on the couch beside Vera, resting her head on Vera's lap. "She knows I'm hurt."

"I'll feed her before I go."

Stin jumped off the couch and followed him into the kitchen.

He hated leaving Vera now, but he had so much to do before the tournament tomorrow. Maybe even call the church to be placed on the prayer chain, something he'd never done before, but he would need all the help he could get.

"If Kevin shows up again, call."

"Ryan, wait."

He stopped in his tracks near the front door. The woman who sat on the couch looked diminutive somehow, as though the injury had knocked her down a peg or two. The usually beautiful and proud Vera looked defeated, and that ripped away at his heart.

"What is it, darlin'?"

He loved the light in her eyes when he called her *darlin'*. For once in his life, he wasn't playing. These feelings were real.

It might be friendship, and it might be true love.

Chapter 11

After a restful night's sleep in her roomy queen- sized bed, Vera decided to ignore the doctor. The next morning she asked Annie to pick her up and take her to the café. Sooner or later, she would find a way to drive with the big boot on her foot, but for now, accepting a ride instead of driving herself was her version of a compromise to the doctor's orders.

"Are you sure about this?" Annie grimaced and stared at Vera's foot. "That looks painful."

"I'll be fine. Besides, I want to keep busy." And keep her mind off Ryan.

After last night, that was hard to do. She kept picturing his smoldering brown eyes and the tender way he'd touched her. Even though he'd had plenty of opportunity, Ryan was always the perfect gentleman.

"How did it happen?" Annie turned the key in the glass door and opened up the silent and dim café. They'd arrived before the sunrise to beat the crowd expected on the way to the slopes to observe or compete.

"A ski accident and my own stupidity." Vera sighed. "I don't know what I was thinking. I should have taken Ryan's offer before this got out of hand."

"His offer?"

"He offered to take my place in the tournament."

Annie smiled. "Wow. Well, I thought he had it bad for you, but I had no idea he was that far gone."

"You're wrong. That's Ryan. He would do this for any one of us. He's the best man I know."

Annie elbowed Vera. "And now I see that it's mutual."

Vera flushed. She'd hoped her feelings were not that obvious. Regardless, a relationship with Ryan was impossible. He deserved someone much better. Someone more like Maggie.

Annie now performed opening tasks with the expertise of someone who had been doing it for years. With an ache, Vera realized that if she was forced to sell the café, Annie would be out of a job, too. *No. Not going to happen.*

"I've been meaning to talk to you," Annie said as she tied on her apron.

"I'm sorry I haven't been around. I'll be here from now on." At least, that was the plan. She hoped one way or another it would happen.

"I've enjoyed working here so much. The locals are some of the nicest people I've ever met. I think I might know the whole town by now."

Everyone said that about Harte's Peak. Even those passing through affectionately called it Little Mayberry.

"In fact, that was how I met the principal of the new private school opening this fall." Annie filled the sink with sudsy water.

"I heard something about that." With so much to do she'd been absent from the weekly Chamber of Commerce meetings, but her e-newsletters had mentioned the private Christian school.

"We really hit it off. She's from Texas,

like I am. Anyway, one thing led to another and she offered me a job starting in the fall," Annie said.

Vera shuffled over to Annie and grabbed her in a bear hug. "I'm so happy for you." Annie had been searching for a teaching job for a long while. Even though Vera would miss her, she couldn't help but be proud that Annie had accomplished her plan.

"I won't have to leave you right away," Annie stared at Vera's foot. "Plenty of time for you to recover."

"Don't worry about me. I'll manage."

"Of course you will. And with a hunk like Ryan on your side, you won't be lonely either," she teased.

"Annie, we're not dating. We're good friends." Very good friends. Hopefully life-long friends.

Annie rolled her eyes, "If you say so."

The morning rush arrived within the hour and kept them both hopping. They worked out a system in which Vera did the least amount of moving, making the drinks while Annie worked the register and also helped fill orders.

Kyle appeared with three young women

he introduced as his snow bunnies. "How's the ankle? I heard about what happened."

"Don't worry about me. You should worry about Ryan," Vera called out from behind the espresso machine.

"I've been meaning to thank you for that. After Ryan entered the contest it finally got interesting." The arrogance might be well placed, but Vera doubted it. Kyle probably saw his easy win evaporating like the steam out of his hot cup of latte.

One of Kyle's bunnies sidled up next to him. "You can listen on the radio. WXPX is going to have live coverage. So you can be among the first to hear about it when Kyle wins."

Vera didn't respond, but she had a radio around here somewhere. She wouldn't miss a minute of the coverage.

After the morning rush, the till was overflowing.

"It's been that way every day," Annie announced.

Vera's spirits buoyed. As she had anticipated, the tournament had been great for business. If only it could be enough. Even so, she'd have to plan adequately for the slow down after the contest. One thing she would never do again is over extend or forget to plan for difficult times.

"Go ahead and enjoy the rest of the day. I can handle things here. I imagine it'll be slow all day. Seems like the whole town has gone out to support the skiers."

"Are you sure?" Annie asked. "I'd love to watch the competition. If you'll be OK."

"Get me the radio, would you? I think it's in the office. I don't want to miss the play by play." Before she left, Annie set everything up for her, including the radio on the counter, tuned to the right station.

She would have to picture Ryan flying down the slopes, his long and steady legs conquering the hill.

A MAJOR PORTION of the population of Harte's Peak had come out to watch the tournament. Great. All the more pressure not to face plant after catching air.

"Ryan, you're a planker? Are you in this race?" Katie, the manager from the bookstore, stood in the viewing aisles with her boyfriend, David, who owned the hardware store in town.

Ryan nodded.

"I'm a last-minute add. I've got to qualify with my time first." Right now, he reconsidered the whole idea. But Vera's face flashed in his mind, the beautiful blue eyes and kissable lips. No, he wasn't giving up.

Kyle approached. "Believe me. He'll qualify. This guy used to be a free rider at heart, like me. He wasn't afraid of anything."

That much was true. Back then he'd used the anger he'd felt against the world to drive him. And until the accident it had worked.

"Lucky for you there's no acro in this competition." Kyle jeered. The acrobatic part of the competition was always where Ryan had been edged out. Linking jumps, flips, and spins were not his style. Pure, unadulterated, freeing speed was his calling card. Always had been.

He made his way through the crowd of well- wishers and joined the line at check-in. The disorganized desk was crowded with contestants yelling out skiers' names as the entrants were assigned random numbers for the first qualifying race. Clearly, the lodge had been unprepared for the overwhelming turnout of amateurs hoping to get a chance at the final race. Not to mention the purse.

Some familiar faces were in the crowd of amateurs, locals who were hoping for a chance at the brass ring. Vera would have been here, but right now he thanked God she wasn't. She was safe at the café, waiting for him to report back with his qualifying times. At least, he hoped they'd be qualifying times.

Lord, help me to do my best. The words of Proverbs 3:4 came back to him. A favorite verse after a particularly long and trying day at work when the occasional thanklessness of his job seeped through to his bones.

Whatever you do, be it in word or in deed, do it heartily as unto the Lord.

Maybe that was what he'd been missing here. Yes, he wanted to do this for Vera, but more than that, he wanted this race to be won for the Lord. And since it would be the first time he'd ever won a race with that in mind, he'd give it everything he had and then some. A downhill race, each contestant would start off alone, a straight shot down the mountain. A digital counter would begin the moment a skier pushed off and end the second they breezed through the finish line.

Like every other amateur hoping to qualify, he'd have three attempts, —and the best times would advance to the final race.

He'd been keeping track of his time on his runs with Vera yesterday, and they had been better than he would have expected.

By his calculations only one prospective amateur out of the crowd would be allowed to place. The rest of the spots would probably be taken by amateurs who were already ranked and more than qualified.

He had to have that spot.

Ryan counted about thirty contestants as together they rode the ski lift to the advanced hill where the first race to the bottom would begin. At the top, they were met by some of the media and officials. The judges were situated about the midway point where they would have the clearest vantage point to the finish line. Even so, they wouldn't be able to see every leg of the competition and would be advised via walkie-talkie from sightseers at different points of the race.

Spectators were gathered below, some holding binoculars and others wearing sunglasses. The early February weather was unnaturally warm and sunny and some in the crowd were already peeling off layers of clothing.

Several amateurs went ahead of him, and Ryan gaged his competition. But this wasn't where his biggest concern lay. If he got the spot, he'd have to contend with Kyle, Shane, and the others.

Finally, his name was announced and Ryan lined up at the starting gate. He fought to keep his focus off the pounding beat of his heart. All he could think about was a day seven years ago when he'd experienced the most agonizing physical pain of his life. When he'd been too full of himself.

Someone from the crowd shouted something which he did not hear and did not care. He held his focus entirely on the next few seconds of his life. *This is it. It's just You and me now, Lord.*

He adjusted his goggles and waited for the signal from the coordinator, heart positioned firmly in his throat. At the sound of the chiming bell indicating it was time, he pushed off. The steady weight distribution on the sole of the outside of his foot gave him the control he required as he raced down the hill, pushing the bottom wind.

Midway through the course he felt the old surge of adrenaline kick in. A strange thing happened—he had a partner in this race, and for the first time in his life he wasn't doing this alone. He'd take care of getting across the finish line, and God would take care of the rest. The cold wind whipped through as he sailed past a tricky turn, catching air.

The swoosh of the skis against the snow, the snow spray whipping against his face, they were all welcome memories. Not the stuff of nightmares. While he'd expected nothing but fearful reminders of the accident, all of that was gone now as he reconciled with an old friend. He could feel the speed, his time had to be good, and as he recognized the last flag before the finish, all doubts were gone.

The crowd roared as he crossed the finish line.

Now the moment of truth. He stared up at the digital clock that would flash his time and listened for the announcer's voice over the speakers.

The time flashed one minute and forty seconds and Ryan winced. In his competitive days, it would have been far from his best score. But today it might just be good enough.

"Time comes in at one minute forty seconds by our very own Deputy Ryan Colton," the announcer's voice rang. "Folks, that's easily a pro's time, which by the way, Ryan used to be. Good luck, everyone. I think this score is the one to beat today."

He found Kyle waiting to congratulate him. "Good job. I think it's safe to say you've got this."

"I'm not counting on it, but I'm pretty happy with that time. Maybe I'll do better next time."

"You'll have to do a lot better if you want to beat me." Kyle flashed a smile. "My last time on a similar course came in at one o' nine. Beat out my competition by a tenth of a second."

"A tenth of a second? That had to hurt."

"Winning is winning. And it's all that matters," Kyle said.

Once Ryan would have thought the same thing, and now he made up his mind to watch Kyle very carefully. Ryan wanted to win again, and even if it was by a tenth of a point, he'd take it.

"Right," Ryan admitted. "See ya later,

I've got two more runs. Who knows? I may get an even better time next. Remember, I've been out of this for a while. But I'm warming up."

He hoped that Kyle heard the challenge in his voice loud and clear. Ryan had a new edge Kyle might never have, or understand. The advantage Ryan had since he realized this was about much more than winning.

By the time the qualifying times of all amateurs seeking to rank were averaged later in the day, Ryan's best time had clocked in at one thirty.

All contestants gathered to hear the final announcement.

"By determination of times, the amateur to advance and hold a spot for the final race will be Ryan Colton."

Ryan was flanked by his friends, many of them clapping him on the back.

In the distance, Kyle raised his thumb in his direction.

Yes, thank you, Lord. By the grace of God he'd taken the spot. Now he only had to win the race.

• • •

VERA WHOOPED when she heard the announcement. Ryan had qualified for the final race. She pulled her cell phone out of her apron, hoping to see a text message or a call. She'd begged him to check in with her at every opportunity, but either reception was lacking on the mountain or he'd been too busy to do so.

Lexi walked in alone and surveyed the empty café.

"Where is everyone?"

"The race. How's your mom?" Vera tried to tone down her enthusiasm.

Ryan had made the qualifying, but the final race would be the biggest challenge. Still, he had a good chance.

She'd seen him fly down that hill first hand. Now all she had to do was pray that he wouldn't get injured in the process of helping her. "Jack sent me here for a triple shot Americano. Mom says he's being a wimp, and that sleep is overrated. She'll have a hot chocolate." Lexi fished through her purse.

"Put your wallet away. This one's on the house." Vera started to fill the order. "How is John?"

"Jack says we don't need the doctor to

tell us that his lungs were fully developed. They let him go home with mom."

The best news she'd had in weeks. John was out of the woods.

Lexi edged closer to the radio. "Is Ryan winning?"

"He just won the spot he needed to be in the final race."

"I can't wait to tell mom and Jack that the race is on the radio. We need to listen to this at home." Lexi rushed out as soon as her orders were ready.

After a few more minutes, the announcer's voice boomed over the radio.

"The line-up of final skiers include Kyle Grant, Ryan Colton, and Shane Zelinski. After a fifteen- minute break the contestants will line up for the last leg…"

Vera didn't hear the rest.

Ryan would soon be lining up for the final leg of the race, an intense run of uneven terrain, and big turns at high speed. This part required not only speed, but precision, to avoid serious injury. Injuries much worse than her broken ankle.

She tried to get Ryan's old accident out of her mind. After all, he'd admitted to being under the influence that time and he no longer drank. Other things could go wrong, though. And she didn't want to think about them.

Instead, she closed her eyes and silently offered up a prayer for Ryan's safety. Since she'd prayed for John, talking to God had become easier.

She pictured Ryan—his beautiful brown eyes, dimpled chin, tender touch—and tears formed in her own eyes. He would do his best, and she no longer cared whether he won, but only that he would be kept safe. *Please God, I won't ask for anything more. Ever again.* The peace she felt after her prayer was quickly disrupted by the sound of the tinkling bell to the door, announcing she had a customer. Opening her eyes, her peace was further shattered by the presence of the man

standing before her.

Kevin.

Vera took a deep breath. Kevin was the last person she wanted to see. Ever.

"Can I help you?" She gnawed at her bottom lip. Better to remain pleasant and not reveal the bitterness that his very presence inspired.

"That's better than your last greeting."

"I don't mean to encourage you." She stared daggers at him.

He held a newspaper under his arm. "That much is clear. I'll have the flavor of the day, whatever it is."

She filled a to-go foam cup with the dregs of the drip coffee and placed it down in front of him, hoping he'd take the hint. "I hoped you'd be gone by now. Haven't you got the message yet? The café will never be for sale."

He ignored her remark. "I see you gave up on the foolish idea of the ski tournament. I'm still interested if you've run out of options. We can talk about it." The man would never give up until he was run out of town. Surely he had better places to be.

"Not quite. You're wasting your time here."

"I'd almost like to know what you have up your sleeve."

"Get used to being disappointed."

"Does your plan have anything to do with that overzealous deputy you hired as security? Bryan— Ryan—what's-his-name? Not necessary and a waste of your money."

She swallowed the hot, burning sensation in her throat. Kevin shouldn't even be allowed to speak Ryan's name. "None. Of. Your. Business."

Kevin carried his cup and newspaper to a table.

"This tournament sounds fascinating."

"It is. Not that it's any of your business."

"Are you kicking me out? Isn't this a free country?" Ignoring her, Kevin settled in.

Even Kevin couldn't ruin this for her. Vera riveted her attention to the radio.

Shane had won the coin toss and was going first.

The announcer began to give a play-by-play.

But only seconds into the race, one of the announcers reported that Zelinski was down.

"Looks like we have an injury, folks. We'll get that information to you as soon as we can. My understanding is that Shane missed a turn and lost his footing. Hopefully, he's OK."

"Speaking of injuries," the other announcer interrupted. "Ryan Colton sustained a nearly deadly injury several years ago that derailed a very promising pro-circuit career."

Vera gripped the edge of the coffee bar

until her knuckles turned white. Why did the announcer have to use the word *deadly?*

A few minutes later, the announcer had news about Shane. "Rescue is on the way. We don't know what kind of condition he's in. We'll report more as we hear, but this has delayed the next contestant."

Kyle was next. Vera backed up against the counter, the wall keeping her from slumping to the ground. Shane was injured. God only knew how badly, and Ryan could be next. After everything they'd both been through, what if all that waited for Ryan was another injury? And it would be her fault.

She stood alone at a time like this—with Kevin. She felt queasy as the room swayed and lurched. Without a doubt, she couldn't hear any more of the broadcast. Couldn't bear to hear any more bad news. With a flick of her wrist she shut the radio off.

Kevin studied her. "I'm confused. Are you seeing Shane or Ryan? I can't keep up. Maybe you can't either. Why don't you just pick one of them?"

She glared at him. "Get. Out."

"Why should I?" Kevin's voice rose. "I have every right to be here."

Kevin's tone, rising in hot anger, caused

Vera's hands to shake. He'd never hurt her physically, but that unspoken threat had always been there. Kevin was an expert at pushing her buttons, and time hadn't changed that. Right now, she was grateful that he was several feet across the room from her and a bar separated them.

"I have the right to refuse service to anyone." She braced against the counter, feeling the words come out through her gritted teeth.

Kevin rose. "But you know better than to refuse me. When I buy this place, I'm going to turn it into a sports bar. Thought you'd like to know."

"You're never getting it. Get it through your thick head."

"Here's what I know. You should have never left me. And I don't care how long it takes. I'm going to make you realize that."

"It's too late. I'm in love with someone else." Even as she said the words meant to discourage Kevin, the realization hit that she was speaking the truth. She loved Ryan, more than she'd ever thought she could love a man.

"I don't believe you." Kevin stared at her through narrowed eyes.

"Believe what you want. You need to leave now, before I call the cops. Ryan isn't the only cop in town, you know." She picked up her cell phone, praying he wouldn't notice her shaking hand.

Kevin snarled. "You know. I would have thought you'd be smarter than to get involved with a cop. What do they make, thirty, forty thousand a year?"

The only thing a bully understands is strength.

From deep inside Vera marshaled every ounce of courage she had left. The woman Kevin had known wouldn't have confronted him, but she'd changed in every way. She wouldn't let him insult Ryan. Not the best man she knew.

Kevin had to get out now or she couldn't be responsible for what she would do. She lifted the radio and threw it in his direction. "Get out. Get out!"

He dodged the radio as it shattered into several pieces on the hardwood floor. "Breaking your own radio. You know what? You're crazy. Have it your way. I'm going."

She half-walked and half-dragged after him and locked the door, turning the sign around.

In her office, she sank to her knees. She

couldn't stop thinking that Ryan might be injured again because of her foolish plan. If only she'd listened and accepted help from the foundation. If not for her misguided idea, he wouldn't have been on the slopes at all. But it was too late. All because of her stupid pride. She needed to pray.

The only Bible scripture that came to mind was one from her childhood. She'd recited it to her mother so many times that it was printed forever on her heart.

The Lord is my shepherd, I shall not want. Though I walk through the valley of the shadow of death, I will fear no evil because You're with me. She had to have some faith.

Like Ryan and Maggie had the night that baby John was born on the side of the highway.

She had to believe that Ryan would be safe. Vera closed her eyes and pictured him flying down the mountain, safe. She didn't care anymore whether he won or not. Only that the man she'd been stupid enough to fall in love with would be all right. She had to let it go and trust in God.

Nothing mattered anymore other than knowing Ryan would be OK. She cradled her cell phone in her hands and waited.

Concentrate. Focus.

As much as he wanted to leave and find out whether Shane's injury was as serious as the announcers kept hinting, Ryan couldn't go anywhere.

The first responders would take care of him, and there'd been enough of a respectful delay in the proceedings.

He stared at Kyle, at the intensity and focus that emanated from him. That's what Ryan needed right now. The edge. He kept grasping for the edge, reaching it and losing it again. The fact remained that he wasn't as single-minded as he used to be, and though that was a good thing, it wouldn't help him win this race.

"I hope he's all right," Ryan said to Kyle's back. Kyle turned to him and adjusted his goggles.

"Yeah. He'll be fine. You were."

Six agonizing months of physical therapy later, he had been. But no one other than his family had known the full story, or the fact that recovering had been the single greatest challenge of his life. Even so, after his body had recovered he couldn't have said the same for his heart. Until the Lord.

Kyle took off in his own inimitable style,

legs firmly planted French fry style for maximum speed. The man was fearless and as he slid down at lightning speed, Ryan knew one thing for certain.

To beat Kyle, he'd have to be every bit as fearless.

When Kyle's speed was announced at one minute twenty seconds, Ryan thought he might have heard wrong. Only ten seconds separated Kyle from Ryan's best time today. For the first time, winning appeared to be a distinct possibility. He could shave off a few seconds of his time if he held the French fry for longer than he had in his previous time. Longer than he felt comfortable.

Ryan positioned himself at the starting line for his attempt. He could do this, with the help of the Lord. After all, he wasn't running this race alone. As he pushed off the hill, feeling the freeing sound of the air rushing past him, he could almost feel the prayers that were with him.

Jack would be praying, and so would Maggie.

Maybe even Vera would be praying, and more than anything else, that caused his spirit to soar.

He was flying now, rounding the turn

with ease, one with the wind. As he crossed the finish line he had no doubts he'd done his best, leaving fear at the gate.

Now, the moment of truth. He turned to stare at the clock and heard the sound of the announcer's voice as the time flashed. One minute, twenty-five seconds. Ryan let out a breath. Good, but not enough. He'd lost to Kyle.

He met Kyle near the end of the trail and shook his hand. "The best man won."

"I don't know about that, bud. But I will say the fastest man won," Kyle said.

"You're faster. By five seconds." Ryan nodded and smiled.

"You had me worried." Kyle laughed. "Thanks for making me work for it."

"Anytime. Just don't spend the money all in one place." It would probably go to fancy dinners and parties, not that he should be one to judge.

"I promise." Kyle winked.

"By the way, before you leave town I do have somewhere I want to invite you." He'd been thinking about asking Kyle to church since he'd seen him, but was unsure of how to approach him. But now, filled with the

Spirit, he wanted to share the peace that he'd found.

The decision would be up to Kyle after that.

A crowd of media and fans soon surrounded them, congratulating Kyle and asking for interviews with both of them. They obliged for a while, taking photos and talking of their past rivalry.

Ryan walked away as soon as he could disengage and left Kyle with the attention he no longer craved. He wanted to apologize to Vera right away, but already the cell reception on the mountain had proved spotty at best. He had no bars on his phone.

Vera would have to move swiftly into Plan B now. He only prayed it wouldn't be too late to get help from the foundation.

As he unfastened his skis and walked toward the lodge, more people along the way turned in his direction and congratulated him on his effort. He asked several people about Shane, but no one seemed to know his exact condition.

He glanced at his phone again. Still no bars. As long as he couldn't reach Vera, he might as well check on Shane.

"How is he?" he called out to rescue personnel.

Today a full medical staff filled the lodge's first aid clinic. Even an orthopedic doctor was on standby.

"Not sure yet. Probably a broken leg. We boarded him, and the doc will make the final call."

Ryan spent a half hour with Shane, as he was assessed by the doctor hired for the event. Once assured Shane would be all right, Ryan prepared to head back to town and check in with Vera. He'd promised to call her right away, and she'd wonder about the results. He wanted to be the one to break the bad news to her, as gently as possible.

"Hey," Tagg said as he grabbed his shoulders.

"You did good."

"Not good enough."

"I was listening to the broadcast on my car radio when I heard the news about Shane. I thought I'd come up and see if I could help."

"It was broadcast?" He had no idea. Now hundreds of people already knew the results. He thought of Vera first and how disappointed she would be. More than any-thing, he hated that he'd let her down.

"How's Shane doing?" Tagg asked.

He stepped aside and pointed in the direction of the clinic, where the doctor was still working on Shane.

"He's going to be fine."

He took out his cell phone again. Still no service. He had to get to Vera.

Chapter 12

Ryan pulled over near the café and glanced at his cell phone. Finally, service again. Dozens of missed calls registered. Jack. Maggie. Lonnie. Calhoun. Vera. *Great, Vera.*

The café's *Closed* sign hung in the doorway, but the lights were still on inside. He went to the door and spied what appeared to be parts of a radio scattered in pieces on the floor.

What had happened in there? Vera wouldn't close up and leave a mess like that. She wouldn't have carelessly left lights on, wasting electricity.

He pulled on the locked doors and considered calling it in. Maybe that ex of Vera's had done something despicable to her.

Some of the evil things he'd seen on the force filled his mind, but he shoved the thoughts out of his head. He sent up a quick prayer for Vera's protection.

Ironic, since she might be feeling a bit worried about his own safety especially given that Shane had been hurt. That kind of news could have been unsettling, as it reminded them all that the sport was not for the faint of heart.

He was about to make a call to the sheriff's station when Vera walked slowly to the front door. Her eyes looked puffy and pink as though she'd been crying. She was either taking this a lot worse than he would have expected, or maybe Kevin had done something to her.

His stomach clenched in fury. He would need help from the Lord to control his temper because right now he wanted to hurt Kevin. Badly.

He smiled, hoping she'd realize that he was all right. A loser, but all in one piece. He held out his arms to the side as though presenting himself. He was fine, and not injured. Other than his pride.

Vera turned the lock and threw open the

door. She grabbed him and wouldn't let go, burying her face in his shoulder.

"You're OK." She sobbed. "When I heard about Shane, I couldn't stop thinking that you might be hurt, too."

"I'm fine, but I came in second. I'm sorry, Vera." He held her close, feeling waves of guilt about enjoying every moment of the way she clung to him.

"Sorry?" She lightly hit his shoulder with her fist.

"You have nothing to be sorry about."

"I didn't win." With his thumb, he wiped a tear away from her cheek.

"I was so scared when I thought you could be hurt. I wish I'd listened to you and never considered this tournament. Will you ever be able to forgive me?" She covered her face with her hands.

"How many times are we going to do this? I'm the one who volunteered, remember? And I'm glad I did. It was actually fun, you know. I'd forgotten how freeing it can be flying down the mountain." The fear gone, he could enjoy skiing again. "I appreciate speed, too. Only I still think it should be kept off the road," he teased.

"I'm an idiot. I should have listened to

you in the first place." She closed her eyes and rubbed he forehead.

"Hey, it's all right. What happened in here?" He stared at the radio pieces on the ground.

She avoided his eyes. "I did that. I lost my temper with someone."

His shoulders tensed. "Kevin?"

"I told him to get out, but he didn't move fast enough. So I gave him an incentive."

"He was here again?" That guy would never get the message.

"Under the pretense of a cup of coffee. Of course he still wants to buy the cafe." She pulled out of his arms, and he resisted the urge to hold her in place.

"And you're still not selling it." He followed her as she walked unsteadily toward the mess on the floor.

"That's what I told him." She bent over to pick up the pieces.

"Sit down. I'll get this." He went ahead of her and pick up the rest. "You and I both need to control our temper."

"Actually, I did. I didn't want to hurt that radio. It was a substitute." Her feeble effort at a smile broke his heart.

"Don't forget. We still have the foundation." This was no longer only Vera's problem. While he wasn't looking, it had become his own.

"Right. I told you I would do that." She looked at the ground.

"Have you?" Why did he get the feeling that she now kept something else from him?

"I haven't yet, but I will. It's that I've been thinking—"

"No. You're not going to bail on me now. You said—"

"I know what I said, but maybe it makes sense."

"What makes sense?"

"To let the bank take back the house. To cut my losses. Start over." She crossed her arms and her thin body seemed to fold in.

"You'd still have your business that way."

"And a black stain on my credit history for years. I can live in an apartment, and some of them will take pets. But I have Stin to think about, and I don't want her trapped in a small apartment all day. You might laugh, and she's not my child, but she may as well be. I need a place for a dog that thinks it's her God-given duty to announce to the world that there's a bird outside."

"I would never laugh about that." Early in his career as a deputy, he'd responded to a call when no one else thought it was important enough. A little kid couldn't catch his dog. Sure, it meant he'd had to stop traffic, something he'd heard about from all the drivers who'd called in the station to complain. The other deputies had ribbed him about it for weeks.

"So if I sell the house, I get to keep my business and my dog. But I lose my home. I lose what I've built."

"You're forgetting that you might not have to lose either one. The foundation might be able to get you back on track."

"And then what? How long can that last? Do I continue to make payments I can't possibly afford on a house that's worth half of what it used to be?"

"Good point. But even if you can't rescue your home, they might be able to help you with the deposit on a rental."

She sighed. "Maybe it's silly, but that house means something to me. It was my independence day. There is no good outcome here."

"Maybe the best outcome is to let it go and give it all over to the Lord." He took her hand, led her to a table and pulled out a chair for her.

"I wish God would tell me what to do." She sat down and rubbed at her legs as though seeking warmth.

"Then ask Him. And then listen for the answer." He'd been listening for answers, too, and it would be nice to have her company.

"I can't do that. I don't know how to pray anymore."

"You seemed to do fine when Maggie asked." Had she forgotten that God had been there with them on the side of the road? That John was fine? The Lord never left them alone, He was always near.

"That's different." Vera worried a nail between her teeth.

"Why?"

"I prayed for an innocent baby. He hadn't done anything wrong. I can't say the same thing for myself."

"There you go again."

God had forgiven Vera, but could she forgive herself?

He'd been there too, only a few months ago.

"I don't want to talk about this." The light in her eyes shifted.

Ryan wouldn't push.

This secret Vera carried could be a time bomb waiting to go off.

Ryan drove Vera home. She wasn't supposed to be driving yet, actually wasn't even supposed to be back at work, but as usual, Vera hadn't listened. He scolded her for not listening to the doctor, but he might as well have held his breath.

He persisted in his attempts to keep Vera off her feet, once literally picking her up and carrying her back to the couch where he ordered her to sit. He found some leftovers in her fridge and warmed them up in the microwave.

"I'm not used to sitting around and being waited on, but I think I like it," Vera said.

"Tomorrow you'll call the foundation?" He didn't want to press too hard, but he had the feeling she planned to avoid the subject again.

"Sure. I will. It's just that—"

"What is it?"

"No matter what you say, the foundation is a church thing and I'm not exactly a good person. Sometimes I wish I could come to God with a clean slate. Start over."

"What makes you think you can't? What do you think I did?"

"Maybe you did, but there are some things that can't be forgiven." Vera looked everywhere but at him.

"No, there aren't. That's the point." He wished he wasn't so young in his own faith.

She needed to talk to someone like Maggie, or Calhoun.

"No, you're wrong."

If Vera had ever discussed this with Maggie, he was sure Maggie would have spoken wisdom into Vera's life.

"What is this terrible thing? Would you tell me?" He leaned in closer.

"No. I can't talk about it." Vera shook her head.

"Have you told Maggie?"

Vera frowned. "Maggie? I couldn't bear the look in her eyes. She might hate me."

"You don't know her very well, then. There isn't a hateful bone in her body."

"OK, she wouldn't hate me, but she would hate what I've done."

"How bad could it be?" He reached for her delicate hand, but she pulled it away.

"I'm not going to tell you, either."

"You're making my imagination run away with all sorts of ideas."

"That's your problem." She folded her arms across her chest.

"Whatever it is, it's not as bad as you think."

"How can you be so sure?"

"Because of you. I know your heart." He locked eyes with hers.

"I'm still not going to tell you." She raised her chin.

"I'm not leaving here until you do." He leaned back on the couch and crossed his arms behind his neck.

Vera glared at him. "You should go now."

Maybe if he stayed, she would tell him. She needed this unburdening. Though he hardly felt qualified to lead her, he could be here for her and listen.

"No. I'm just as stubborn as you are."

"I hope you don't have any other plans, because you're going to be here for a while." Vera tugged at a lock of her hair.

"Fortunately, I don't have to work until tomorrow night." He settled in, making a show of getting comfortable by reaching for the remote.

"You're not my friend if you make me do this." She rocked back, clutching her waist.

"Maybe I'm a friend if I do. You need to tell someone. Why not me? You already know my past demonstrates I'm no saint."

"Fine." Vera got up and hobbled into one of the back rooms of the house. Stin followed close behind.

"Where are you going now?"

She came out with a small shoebox and placed it in his lap.

"What's this?"

"Open it. You want to know so badly." Her blue eyes filled with tears.

He took the lid off and found a silver baby rattle, a pink hair bow, and a small and delicate pink blanket.

"I don't understand."

"That's all I have left of my baby. I killed my baby, Ryan. Is your God big enough to forgive that?"

SHE COULDN'T BEAR to look at Ryan anymore. His face would reflect the hatred she had for herself. A good man like him would hate what she'd done. But as much as it hurt to do it, after what he'd done for her he deserved to know the truth. There was a very good reason she didn't deserve anyone's charity, much less that of a church.

"These things belonged to your baby?" Ryan finally asked.

"They were the first and only things I bought when I found out I was pregnant. She died before I could buy any more."

"When did this happen?" His eyebrows furrowed, a pained look in his eyes.

Her throat grew raw with unshed tears. She'd thought enough tears had been shed over the years, but no matter what, when she brought out the box there were still more.

"I was eighteen and modeling in Europe. You'll remember that my mother let me go without a chaperone. I met a young man. I fell in love, or so I thought. And then, well, by the time I realized I was pregnant I was about three months along. I was excited, but you can imagine the modeling agency was upset. They threatened to cancel my con- tract, threatened to tell my mother. You know what they wanted me to do."

"Is that what you did?" His gaze held

nothing but compassion as he pulled her down on the couch beside him.

"No, it's what I told them I would do. I thought if I had more time I could figure out a way to keep the baby. Of course, the boy didn't want to have anything to do with it. I knew how upset my mother would be, but I finally told her over the phone. All she did was berate the agency for not supervising me better. I refused to do what they told me to, but as it turned out, it happened anyway. I miscarried about four months."

"How is that your fault?"

"Because I didn't take care of myself the way I should have. I didn't even know for the first three months, and I should have. I stayed thin for the runway. I didn't feed my body properly so it wasn't a hospitable environment. I think those were the words the doctor used." Her womb. Inhospitable.

"Darlin', that's not your fault." There was such love in his eyes it undid her. Again, he untangled her pain with his big heart.

"Whose fault is it, then? I was the one who should have taken better care of my body. Then maybe my baby would have lived. A little girl. I asked."

"Come here." Ryan pulled her into his

arms, and she didn't protest. The pine tree scent of him warmed her heart —a heart she kept forgetting to guard around him. Already he had broken through her toughest wall.

"During our marriage, Kevin found out about the miscarriage. He used it against me. When I couldn't become pregnant, he blamed my defective womb. I had to accept the fact that maybe I'm not meant to be a mother."

"This is why you told me that some people shouldn't be parents? That you never want kids?" Ryan whispered in her ear.

She couldn't speak any more through her tears. And because she loved Ryan she couldn't be with him. She'd already seen his arms filled with a baby and he deserved that kind of happiness more than anyone else she'd ever known.

A family. And a wife who could give him one.

IT TOOK the better part of a week to stop thinking of the tournament loss. Ryan hadn't been the one hurt in the tournament. But later, after holding an anguished Vera in his arms, his heart hurt for her. He'd take a broken leg like Shane's any day.

Without knowing what to do, he'd held her in his arms until she'd fallen asleep. Then he'd left her on the couch, covered with a blanket, and slipped off for home.

For the next few days he'd felt raw, like someone had turned his skin inside out. And, yeah, maybe he'd been a tad overprotective. He'd driven Vera to work every day until, with a smirk, she'd threatened to file a restraining order. He'd gotten the message.

Now that the tournament was over and Vera swore she'd never step foot inside a gym again, he missed seeing her every day.

He hadn't let Kyle leave without asking him to church, but Kyle had too many excuses for not attending. Perhaps feeling some amount of guilt, Kyle had left a considerable donation to the foundation. As much as Ryan appreciated that, it wouldn't make a dent in the overwhelming needs of the community. It seemed that more foreclosure notices were issued every day. And the foundation couldn't help all of them with its current funding.

Vera's paperwork application for the foundation grant had gone through. Their pro-bono lawyer had explained that they were working with the bank and trying to negotiate terms.

He couldn't get any more information because the process had to be confidential, and even though he worked for the foundation, he wasn't entitled to know every detail.

He did know that another application had come through at the last minute. Mrs. Jones, Harte's Peak only centenarian, had been scammed by a fly-by-night lender who'd pulled up stakes and left town. She could also lose her home, a home owned by some member of the Jones family since before the founding of Harte's Peak.

They were all working diligently to organize fundraisers and phoning for donations.

Ryan prayed that somehow there would be enough money raised to help both of them. Now he sat at his desk at the end of a long day, writing out a report of the day's activities.

Jack came in from patrol. He looked ragged, with bloodshot eyes and dark circles under his eyes.

"How's it going?" Jack asked. They never had much of a chance to talk anymore since their shifts often overlapped.

"I should ask you. Do you sleep at all?" Ryan laughed.

"I've learned to sleep standing up if I have to. A few minutes here, or there. Never through the night, though. Maggie said it might be another two months."

"Sounds like torture. You do know sleep deprivation is one of the tools used on enemy combatants. To break them down."

"I can see why. I'd do almost anything for a few more minutes. Pathetic." He picked up the coffee carafe and poured a cup. "I've been meaning to ask you. Whatever happened to that Kevin guy, the one who kept parking in tow-away zones?"

"Guy has the worst luck I've ever seen. Pretty sure he left town after the second time his Rolls was towed away." Sometimes the lack of parking in a small town was a good thing.

After Kevin's last visit to the café, he'd been issued a ticket every other day.

He had a feeling they wouldn't be seeing Mr. Wall Street again anytime soon.

"How's Vera? Is the foundation going to come through?"

"Think so. The only problem is that Mrs. Jones needs help, too."

"Mrs. Jones? I thought she owned that house free and clear."

"She got scammed by one of these lowlife companies."

"Will there be enough funds for both?"

"That's what we hope. Calhoun is already talking about another bachelor auction. Only this time we have one less bachelor." Two years ago, they'd managed to raise several thousand dollars to help start a small free health clinic in town.

"Yeah, I'm off the market."

"Ever since the first time you saw Maggie, I would say."

Jack laughed. "Well not quite, but yeah."

"Sometimes I wish I could say the same. I get tired of being alone."

"It isn't easy."

"I said I wouldn't ask anyone out until I thought there was a chance she could someday be my wife. And now, I can't stop thinking of Vera." But even though she seemed to be navigating her way back to her faith, he could never keep up with her lifestyle. Not on his public servant salary.

"There's a surprise. Maggie has thought for a while you two are perfect for each other. I do love my wife, but it's annoying when she's always right."

"Vera is a good friend. That's all she thinks of me."

"Are you sure?"

"Do you actually think Vera could ever be happy with someone like me?" He didn't want to spell it out for Jack. Neither one of them made enough money. Even though what was enough was different depending on the person, certainly he would never make enough for his wife to buy designer shoes. Not by a long shot.

"Why not?"

"I thought you'd be the first to discourage me.

Vera isn't exactly a church-going girl."

"I'd be the last person to tell you that." Jack shook his head. "I wasn't a Christian when I met and fell for Maggie. But she had the patience to wait for me to find out for myself. Remember?"

"How could I forget? You would read from the Bible at your desk. And then ask me if I'd ever heard that before."

"Sometimes love is just--love." He shrugged.

"And you can't help who you love."

"Something like that."

Ryan couldn't help the way he felt, and rarely a day had gone by that he didn't picture those piercing blue eyes returning his gaze. Or remember the feel of the silky blonde hair in his fingers. He could almost see the reflection of their future children in her eyes. But that was crazy.

Chapter 13

Baby John looked like a plump roast with one month of growth under him. His cheeks were chubby and rosy pink. His hair was a golden brown, almost the exact color of Jack's.

"What are you feeding this kid? He's growing like a weed." Vera peered at him as he slept in Maggie's arms.

"All he does is eat and sleep. Too bad he has his days and nights mixed up," Maggie yawned.

"You looked drained. Is there anything I can do to help?" She didn't want to hold John again and feel his precious soft skin. It hurt too much, but Maggie looked worn out.

After her talk with Ryan the walls had

come crumbling down. She'd cried off and on for a week. Then she'd hidden the box in the back of her closet, deep behind all the shoes she'd accumulated over the years. He didn't hate her after hearing what she'd done. It still surprised her, but his acceptance also made her consider letting Maggie know why she didn't want to hold her baby.

"I'm kind of leashed to him since I'm the only one who can feed him."

Vera sighed with relief. There were probably a million other things she could do for Maggie while she put up her feet and relaxed with the baby. After all, her ankle had improved and the boot would come off sooner than planned. In the meantime she'd managed a delicate balance with her movements and no longer had to hop around and avoid placing any weight on it.

"I'll take care of these dishes." The sink was full.

Jack was at work and Lexi at school.

"That would be awesome. It's sometimes hard to even get in the shower." Still in a bathrobe at eleven o'clock, Maggie looked overwhelmed.

"I can't help you with that." Vera smirked.

She hadn't held the baby since they'd been in the hospital, but fortunately Maggie appeared too sleep- deprived to notice.

"What's going on with the foundation?" Maggie yawned.

"All the onerous paperwork has been turned in, and I'm waiting. Of course, I missed another month so the bank is constantly hounding me. I screen all my calls. I don't know what else I can do."

"Have you seen Ryan lately?"

Ryan. She missed him so much. The scariest thing about loving him was realizing it with such certainty and knowing they couldn't be together. "I don't see him as much as I used to. I refuse to go back to that torture house he calls a gym, and I've been good about keeping to the speed limit, so other than his occasional trips to the café, I never see him."

"I'm sure he's busy, too. I hate to mention it, but another place you could see him would be church."

"I'm aware of that." She hadn't told anyone, but she'd started reading the Bible again. If she told Maggie she'd probably cry tears of joy so she planned to hold back the news until she had more of it to give.

"Unless, of course, you're happy about not seeing him anymore." Maggie caressed her baby boy's face.

"No. I guess I'm not happy about that. But that's the way it has to be."

"But why?" Maggie met her eyes, a look of worry etching the angles in her face.

"We're not right for each other."

"Hmmm, well I happen to disagree. But I think you know that."

"Don't start playing matchmaker. Didn't you see Ryan holding your baby at the hospital? That's what he deserves to have someday—a family."

"I know you're nervous around babies, but surely John has changed your mind? I mean, he was born in the backseat of your car in the winter and look how well he's doing. Babies are resilient." Maggie kissed his little nose.

Maybe if they're given enough time to grow in the safety of their mother's womb. She didn't say another word and concentrated on scouring a particularly difficult pan in which someone, probably Maggie, a terrible, though well-meaning cook, had burned rice.

"If you love Ryan, and I think maybe

you do, why couldn't you be the one to give him a family?"

Though John slept on, Maggie continued to coo and rock him.

The loving sounds of a mother with her child undid Vera. All the words of her story poured out like water from the faucet. She'd told Ryan and he didn't hate her. He didn't call her a monster. So now she told Maggie.

Maggie sobbed. "Why didn't you tell me? You were a kid. You didn't know any better."

"But you did. You were my age when you got pregnant with Lexi."

Maggie put John down in the baby bouncer and hugged Vera. "I had my mother. She was my biggest support until she passed away. And Lexi's dad was a good father who didn't walk away from us. We had two very different stories. Don't try to compare them."

Once again, Vera was reminded of how she didn't have a real mother. Not one whose support she could count on. Maybe that was the real reason she didn't want to be a mother herself. She didn't have a good example to follow. She'd never had motherly love modeled for her. And she still longed to have that relationship with her mother, no matter how many years passed.

"You're right. I blamed my mother as much as I blamed myself. None of it has done me any good."

"I still can't believe you didn't tell me this before."

"I'm sorry. Ryan was the first person I ever told."

"Ryan?" Maggie's eyes grew wide.

"What can I say? He had me in a tough spot and he wouldn't give up. So stubborn."

"Yeah, sounds like someone else I know." Maggie winked.

"We used to be alike. But he's changed, and I have to admit I want what he has."

"You can have that, too. Do you think this is some exclusive club membership or something? There's no secret handshake. You're in anytime you want to be a member of God's family."

"I'm not like you. I've made more mistakes than I care to think about. And thanks to that, I may never be able to have a baby of my own."

"But why?"

"After the miscarriage, I had an infection. And I've never been able to get pregnant since then. While I was married, we tried. Of course he blamed me."

"Maybe he's the one who can't have children."

"No, we both got tested. And they couldn't find anything wrong with either one of us. But I know it must be my fault. It's my penance for what I've done."

"All I want is for you to know that no matter what you've done, our God is big enough to forgive you."

"You've always looked on the bright side, but there are no rainbows and unicorns here."

Maggie rolled her eyes. "No, there's a lot of pain and suffering where there doesn't have to be. I love you, and I'm tired of seeing you drown in the hurt. Sooner or later, you have to believe that even if you can't forgive yourself, God can."

More than anything, she wanted Ryan to be happy, someday holding his own child in his arms. And that was something she couldn't give him, however much she wanted.

Ryan thought he was seeing things when he noticed the pale blonde hair of the woman sitting next to Maggie at church, but as she walked out of church the black boot was a dead give-away. Vera was attending church with Maggie and her family. The last time he'd seen her here had been Christmas time.

She smiled as she saw him near the exit to the sanctuary. "Don't look so shocked."

"This is not my shocked face. If you want to see that face, you should see what I look like when the cookies are already gone by first service." Ryan grinned.

Maggie, Jack, and Lexi followed close behind. Jack held his sleeping son in his arms.

"Ryan, do you mind giving Vera a ride home? We have to go by the store and I don't want to hold Vera up," Maggie said.

"But…" Vera began, and then a look of understanding reached her eyes and she smiled. "Of course. I guess I need a ride, Deputy."

"Sure," He locked gazes with Vera. The Butler family waved good-bye. Vera sighed. "She can't help herself."

If he got to be on the receiving end of Maggie's efforts today, he considered himself blessed. "I'm not complaining."

Vera's face blushed pink, not a usual occurrence.

"Do you mind if we check something out first before we go?" Last week he'd found a stray cat hanging around the back of the church property. He'd been helping supervise the youth group's baseball game when he'd noticed the scrawny looking stray.

They walked to the back of the portables that served as meeting places for youth and Bible study groups and found the stray waiting under a bush.

Ryan motioned for Vera to sit on the picnic table bench and joined her.

The cat walked tentatively toward Ryan as though he already recognized him.

He pulled out a bag of treats he'd brought in his jacket and started to feed the little animal. "Do you want to feed him?" He offered a few of the treats to Vera.

A pained looked crossed Vera's face. "He's so sickly looking. I wonder what happened to him."

"He probably got separated from the others. Who knows? He looks like the runt, for sure. I know eventually I'll have to take him in to the pound, but first I'm trying to get him fattened up. He has a better chance of being adopted then."

Vera took a treat and tenderly fed it to the weak cat. "You poor thing."

"If you think he looks bad now, you should have seen him last week."

The cat finished its food, cleaned himself, and went to nap under the bush again.

It was a beautiful, early spring day. The chill of winter still hung in the air as the sun beamed with a promise of things to come. He was in no hurry to take Vera home.

"I named him Hercules."

"That name hardly fits."

"I wanted to encourage him." He shrugged.

"You shouldn't have named him."

"Why not?"

She brushed wispy stray hairs out of her eyes.

"Hurts less when you have to give him up."

He hadn't been able to get his mind off Vera since she'd told him about her miscarriage. But they hadn't spoken of it again. He wanted her to know that he didn't judge her. That he thought many people had failed her and he didn't plan on being one of them.

"You never told me what your mother did after you lost the baby."

She looked at the ground. "Nothing."

"Nothing? Didn't she come out to be with you, send for you, anything?"

"No, that's not her style. I got a note telling me to keep my chin up. These things happen for a reason. Someday the time will be right. I'll have another chance. Blah, blah, blah." She folded her arms in front of her.

He shook his head. He couldn't believe a mother would be so cold. His mother had been just the opposite, doting to the point of suffocation. Until now, he hadn't realized how blessed he'd been.

"Did you ever ask her why she did that?"

"Of course not. What would be the point?"

"The point is she should answer for that."

"You're dreaming, Ryan. My mother doesn't answer to anyone."

"Well, maybe she should." He took her hand and this time she did not pull away.

They both remained silent for a few minutes.

He broke the silence because he needed

to tell her now. He didn't want to do it, but he had to. "I heard that Mrs. Jones is about to lose her home as well." Still holding her hand, he avoided her eyes.

"Mrs. Jones? I thought she owned her home for eons."

"I guess she did. What I heard is that the house needed work. You can imagine, because the house is older than the town itself. So she got a loan against it, but it wasn't a legitimate company. Basically, it was a swindle."

"Who would do that to an old lady?" Her hand tightened around his.

"I don't know, but I'd like to meet them some day in a dark alley. OK, I'm kidding. Still."

"The foundation is helping her, as well?"

"That's the thing. We might not have enough money raised to help both you and Mrs. Jones."

Vera fell silent.

"But don't worry. Your application came in first."

She let go of his hand. "Ryan, I don't want to take money away from Mrs. Jones."

"I said there might not be enough, but the church has been planning a big fundraiser for weeks. Tomorrow, a popular Christian band, Greatest Gift, is performing free of charge. We're going to charge for entry as a donation and we already expect a large crowd."

She eased off the bench and walked several paces away. "If there isn't enough money, Mrs. Jones can have it all. I'll find another way. Or I'll let it go."

His heart sank. After all the effort and her stubbornness in regard to charity, it was coming down to this. Not enough money. Why was that always the story?

He came up behind her, put his arms around her waist, and pulled her close. He spoke softly in her ear.

"Don't do this darlin'. It will work out."

She leaned in to him. "Take me home. I don't know how much longer I'll have one."

He wanted to tell her as long as he was alive she would have a home, but he didn't want to make any empty or overblown promises. That Ryan was long gone. He turned her around in his arms. "As long as you promise to come with me to the concert tomorrow night."

"I should have known you'd be there."

"I volunteered for security. What else?"

"You're the bouncer?" She cracked a smile.

"This will be the easiest security work in the world. These are all good kids."

"OK, but it's not a date. It's two good friends hanging out together."

He tried to pretend it didn't hurt. This would have been his first date in months. "Whatever you say."

She started walking toward the parking lot and away from him.

His heart reminded him that he might have to get used to that.

Vera thought it would be less like a real date if she drove her own car, so she insisted on meeting Ryan at the concert the following night. The look in his eyes when she'd told him this wouldn't be a date had pained her. He'd have a much better chance at happiness with any one of the women who gazed longingly in his direction any time she cared to notice.

An uncomfortable feeling settled in the pit of her stomach every time she noticed their dreamy looks in his direction.

A long line of cars snaked through the entrance to the church. Ryan hadn't been kidding. A crowd close to the size of their town would be here tonight. The sanctuary had been turned into a small concert hall for the night.

She'd never heard of Greatest Gift and even though a country music girl at heart, if the event raised money for the foundation, she would happily support it. Besides, she couldn't kid herself anymore. She had little willpower when it came to being with Ryan. She'd fallen in love with him. Her own fault. And even though she tortured herself by prolonging the inevitable, she couldn't help it.

She recognized some friends. Former Sheriff Calhoun was manning the ticket booth.

Vera thought she saw Lexi with a tall, skinny man- boy. She made a mental note to make sure Maggie knew that her daughter was here with a boy, but at the same time realized Lexi would be foolish to show up with someone not approved by her parents. There were probably a hundred gazes on the stepdaughter of the town's current sheriff. The poor thing.

"Excuse me, miss. May I see your ticket stub?" Vera turned.

Ryan stood beside her. "We don't want anybody sneaking in."

"Then you should have hired a bouncer," Vera joked.

Ryan winced and held his chest as though he'd been injured. "Ouch. Usually women put the knife right in my back."

Vera laughed. "Hurry up and show me to my seat.

I don't have all day."

His arm on her back, he led her in the direction of the sound booth near the back of the sanctuary. "You and I have special seating. We can sit with the sound man. It's a much better view of the show."

The cushioned seat was much more comfortable than the folding metal chairs they'd brought in. And from this height she had a great view of Lexi and the boy. She decided she didn't particularly like the way he clung to her waist.

"Excuse me for a minute. I'm still on the clock and besides, I promised Jack I'd check this kid out." Ryan hooked his finger in the direction of Lexi's affectionate friend.

Ryan skillfully sidled up next to Lexi and the boy and made his presence known. The boy quickly let go of Lexi. Poor girl was going to have a hard time holding on to a boyfriend with Jack and his deputies protectively guarding her, but in the long run, that was a good thing. Whoever was serious enough to stick around would likely be a keeper.

Ryan talked to Lexi and the boy, and after a few minutes they were all laughing together. He had a similar sort of relationship with many of the young people, all of whom seemed to know and respect him.

With a pang, Vera realized that even some of the younger girls gave Ryan dreamy eyes. The fact that he appeared completely oblivious to it made her love him even more.

The music began. This concert was about much more than the smooth, lilting voices as they rose in harmony accompanied by exemplary musicians. The lyrics told the story in worship and praise. She recognized many of them as verses straight out of the Bible.

Ryan returned to his seat and leaned closer to her.

"I guess King David was a pretty good songwriter. His lyrics have lasted thousands of years."

Vera had her eyes riveted to the female

drummer who had made her way to the front of the stage. The music continued with a light strumming of guitars and piano. But as the girl stood behind the microphone, a hush fell over the theater.

"'For I am persuaded that neither death nor life, nor angels nor principalities nor powers, nor things present nor things to come, nor height, nor depth, nor any other created thing can separate us from the love of God that is in Christ Jesus our Lord.' A while ago, I didn't think I was good enough. I was the one who separated myself from Christ, not the other way around. I'd done so many terrible things and hurt so many of the people who loved me that I didn't think I could ever be forgiven. I let myself drown in a sea of drug addiction because I thought that's all I deserved. In some ways, I waited for death. I didn't realize I was already dead. But because of Christ, I have been released from bondage. I'm alive again in Him. Amen. And if Christ can forgive someone like me, He can forgive you, too."

Applause fill the auditorium as the young girl took her place back at the drum set and the songs resumed.

Vera trembled from the inside out. A

strange feeling had come over her. Between tears and joy, her body tingled with an electric charge.

Memories of her baby girl came flooding back, of the grief she'd never fully expressed. Now, at this concert of music, possibly the best sermon she'd ever heard preached. All the heartbreak, grief and loss too long buried rose to the surface. It was time to face the past. If not now, it might never happen. She realized this as certainly as she breathed, while she tried to calm her quivering legs.

The timing left something to be desired, but then again, God had his own clock.

"Are you all right?" Ryan put his hand on hers as the concert ended.

"I'd like you to take me somewhere. Now."

Chapter 14

The concert ended and the sun began to slip down the mountain.

Ryan drove Vera to the valley. Vera had asked him to drive her to her mother's house in Sonoma, and though he had a few questions, he didn't want to refuse.

She'd looked incredibly fragile when she'd asked, as though she might break in two, her blue eyes glistening with unshed tears. Her bottom lip trembled slightly.

No, he didn't want her to drive there alone.

"Why is now the time to see your mother?"

"Because I can. If I wait, I'll chicken out."

He understood that too well, though it didn't quite fit with what he knew about Vera. "Brave Vera? Chickening out?"

"I haven't always been brave, you know."

"You could have fooled me."

"Something about my mother makes me shake in my medical boot."

He grinned.

Even now, she was able to see the lighter side of the matter.

The moments that lay at her mother's door were not going to be emotional fluff, and he steeled himself for what might be ahead.

The stately home was in an older established subdivision of town and reeked of wealth.

Would Vera ask her mother for money? It made sense, and he hoped that she would at least consider it.

He'd been encouraged by the turnout tonight, but it still looked smaller than they'd expected since the community's needs kept growing.

Ryan pulled into the circular driveway and glanced at his watch. The drive had taken approximately two hours and darkness had descended on this March evening.

No lights were on inside the house.

"Are you sure she's home?"

"My mother is almost never out after seven. It's dark because she hordes electricity. She's probably in the back room." Vera jumped out of his car. Within seconds, she pounded on the door with purpose.

He walked behind her, unsure of his role. "Do you want me to wait outside?"

"No. You should come in." She looked out of breath.

He wanted to calm her down.

She had to do this and he couldn't stop her.

The frail woman who opened the door didn't remind him much of her daughter. Instead of Vera's pale blonde tresses, Vera's mother's hair was jet black.

"Vera, what on earth?" The woman gripped her housecoat at the neck.

"Mom, I have to talk to you right now. It's important." Vera pushed past her and he followed.

"Who are you?" She stepped away from Ryan.

"I'm Ryan Colton, ma'am." He held out his hand, but Vera's mother showed no inclination to greet him with a handshake. He stuck his hands in his jacket.

"He's my friend, Mom. Ryan, this is my mother, Ava Carrington."

Even the name sounded old world and sophisticated.

Mrs. Carrington harrumphed under her breath.

"What are you—six feet? Six one?"

"Six two, ma'am." He had no idea what his height had to do with anything.

It wasn't as if he'd *accomplished* his height.

"Of course. Vera likes tall men," Ava said.

"Never mind that, Mom. Can we talk?" Vera asked.

"What's so important to bring you down your precious mountain at this time of the night?"

"It's seven thirty." Vera folded her arms.

"It's dark. That's all I know." Mrs. Carrington made her way into what looked like a formal living room.

Ryan followed, unsure of himself. He wanted to sit outside the living room and give them their privacy, but he also didn't want to take liberties in this mausoleum. He waited for some direction.

"I've put everything away, but we can have some tea if you'd like. Young man? Would you like some tea?" Mrs. Carrington sighed.

"No, ma'am. I'm fine."

"We won't be here that long," Vera added.

"Why? What's this all about? And what on earth happened to your foot?" As though she'd just now noticed it, Ava stared at Vera's boot.

"I hurt it, but I'm fine."

"Well, it would have been nice to get a call. I do want to know when my children are hurt, you know."

"I didn't want to bother you."

"Of course not." Ava pursed her lips. "You never do."

"I'm here to tell you that it wasn't right to let me stay in Europe after I lost the baby."

Ava sat up straighter and looked with intensity in Ryan's direction. "This is not a subject I'll talk about with a stranger in the room."

Vera glanced at Ryan. "Would you please wait in the foyer?"

The wildly emotional look in her gaze

made him reluctant to leave her. He nodded and retraced his steps back to the foyer.

Vera closed the doors that separated the living room, and he listened as the voices inside grew louder and more insistent. Ava appeared as cold and unemotional as he imagined she would be. A woman with a somewhat vacant look in her eyes.

He distracted himself by admiring the two framed pictures that sat on the small table. The one of Vera may have been from a modeling assignment. She looked other-worldly beautiful in a flowing royal blue gown. And in her eyes he glimpsed the freedom and joy of youthful innocence. He'd do almost anything to put that look on her face again.

The other photo was presumably of her sister, Amy, and looked to be some type of graduation photo. Amy took after their mother, which could only mean Vera took after her father. The man who'd left the family. In a much older photo of the three of them, obviously taken in a studio, Ava sat regally between her two young daughters. Though she didn't look like Vera, Ava Carrington had also been a stunningly beautiful woman in her youth.

He paced the small foyer, praying silently and listening to the sound of Vera's sobs. His hands turned into fists inside his jacket, and he fought to restrain from coming in after her. Something had happened to her at the concert. If he had to guess, he would say that Vera was about to spill it all out—all her secrets, all her pain—and let the chips fall where they may.

Vera talked through her sobs, and had not realized it could be so liberating. All of the agony and grief after the miscarriage came rushing forward, and she poured it all out before the woman who should have been there for her.

Her mother stared at her, slack-jawed. "What do you expect me to say?"

"How about I'm sorry?"

"All right. I'm sorry. In my day, we didn't talk about everything over and over again until we ran it into the ground the way all you young people want to do. What good is it to talk about it? Does it take the pain away?"

Mom was right about that much. The pain wasn't gone, but somehow it was lighter, like it had longed to come out of hibernation in her soul. "You never wanted to talk about any of it. But it does help. Believe it or not."

"It never helped me." Ava frowned.

"And another thing. Kevin isn't the great guy you think he is." For the next few minutes she related what her marriage had been like behind closed doors, how Kevin had fooled everyone, even their congregation.

Ava held her hand to her chest. "But all those things—Kevin said it was a big mistake."

"And you wanted to believe him. I don't know why. I'm your daughter, Mom. You should have supported me. I thought I loved Kevin, but now that I know what love is, I can recognize a counterfeit."

"Now you know what love is?" Ava asked.

"I do. And I know that I love you. I always will." Vera drew closer to her mother and hugged her, the way she had as a child when the only thing she'd ever been angry about was not being able to have a second piece of cake for dessert.

Her mother's embrace surprised her, almost making her draw back, but Vera clung to her.

"I love you, too," Mom whispered.

"I forgive you. You did the best you could." Vera touched her mother's hair, a once luxurious mane of thick black hair, now thinning as the gray roots pushed through the black dye.

Mom had taught her daughters to always be proud of their appearance, but she hadn't concentrated much on the inside.

Vera rose to open the living room doors and found Ryan waiting.

"Is everything OK?" he asked.

She went into his open arms, where she wished she could remain forever. It felt so safe here, but she had to stop being so selfish. "I'm good."

He rubbed her back. "Then let's go. We have a long drive back."

"Thank you for bringing her. I hope I see you again," Mom said.

"Nice meeting you," Ryan said.

He opened the front door and waited for Vera to go through first, ever the gentleman.

"That didn't take long, did it?"

"You could have taken as long as you needed. It sounded important." He opened the door to the car for her.

"Yes, it was. A long time coming."

They were treated to a bountiful display

of stars as they ascended into the mountains and away from the city lights.

"Let's pull over and look at the stars when we get to town. That is, if you have time," Vera said.

"I always have time for you." His strong warm hand reached for hers.

He pulled over at Starlight Park near the cliff. They sat on the hood of his truck, leaning back on the windshield while every star in the sky winked her a welcome home.

"God's creation." Vera sighed.

He pulled her into his arms. "Exactly. God makes beautiful things. Including you."

Vera tensed. It was the first time he called her beautiful. Before she'd always felt it was a line, the first thing guys noticed about her, without bothering to see anything beyond that.

That wasn't Ryan and something in his eyes told her he felt her beauty was more than skin deep.

For once, she could believe it, too.

He turned to face her. In his smoldering brown eyes she forgot that he deserved more than she could give him.

When Ryan kissed her as though he held the most precious thing in his life she felt centered for the first time since she could remember. His kiss was tender, passionate, loving. She couldn't stop kissing him back. This was love, and she knew it with the certainty that the sun would rise again in the morning. For the first time in her life, she knew what it was like to truly love a man. It would break her heart when she had to say good-bye.

WATCHING the stars on the hood of his car with Vera in his arms was certainly not something he'd imagined doing. The old Ryan had been slain by her obvious beauty, but now he'd seen firsthand the kind of heart that beat inside this wonderful woman.

His dreams would never have measured up to this reality of Vera in his arms, the sky above them declaring the glory of the one God who still looked out for him. It appeared the future the Lord had imagined for him was greater than anything he could have thought of on his own.

He didn't want to move or go anywhere else, but as the hour grew late Vera began to shiver in his arms. The cold night mountain air was upon them. He took off his jacket and placed it around Vera's shoulders.

"We should get back," Vera finally spoke. "I have to open up the cafe in the morning. I promised Annie." He hopped off the car, took her hand, and helped ease her off the hood. He still worried about that foot, even though Vera acted as though she was fully healed.

As they rode the short distance back into town Vera remained quiet.

"I know this wasn't a date, but whatever it was, it's the best time I've had in a long time." Even sitting in the foyer and listening to Vera sob had been worth the time spent with her. He was grateful for the ability to take care of her.

"It still wasn't a date," Vera said.

"No, I'd like to think I could do better than star gazing. I do have a job, you know. I can afford to pay for your dinner and everything."

In the last few minutes an enormous wall had risen up between them. As they pulled up into the driveway of her home, he shut off the car.

Vera didn't move, and he allowed her the silence.

She looked at the floor, to him, and back to the floor.

His heart jumped in surprise. He was no idiot. He was about to be dumped. By a girl who wasn't even his girlfriend. He steeled himself, but found that he could not put up walls anymore. Not with Vera. "What is it, darlin'?"

"I'm sorry. I can't. You know there is something going on between us."

"I kind of got that feeling."

"You weren't wrong to feel that way. But the truth is, Ryan, you and I both know we're not right for each other."

"I don't know that."

"I know it. Trust me with this."

"Shouldn't I have a say, too?"

"You wouldn't make the decision with your head. You would do it with your big heart." She touched his chest with her right hand, and he felt branded.

"I'm not the only one with a big heart, darlin'." He placed his hand over hers.

"You're not the right man for me. I know it's true." And suddenly he got it. He recalled the elegant taste in clothes and homes, the remarks her ex-husband made. He'd ignored the truth and all the signs, maybe because he wanted to. He wasn't ever going to make enough money to suit her. Not on a public servant's salary.

"I get it. A cop doesn't make enough money for the lifestyle you've become accustomed to."

Her eyes narrowed, and she looked about to protest.

He would love to have an argument with her. Hash things out and get to the bottom of it all. But a look of resignation crossed her face.

"You're right."

He felt his fists tighten. How could he have been so incredibly wrong about her?

She had admitted it.

He couldn't very well argue with the evidence straight in front of him, as much as he wanted to believe otherwise.

"Someone like Kyle is probably more up your alley." He couldn't help the dig. While he thought he was over his childish rivalry with Kyle, she'd brought it back up front and center.

"Right." Vera turned away and opened the door.

"Good night, Ryan."

She got out of his car and walked away while his heart found a place in his throat.

The anger rose inside of him again, that hostility he'd thought long buried. He needed a punching bag because he wanted to hit something right now. Hit it hard.

Vera would have never thought Ryan would come up with the perfect reason to turn him down. The fact that he'd believed it so easily was only a little painful. She'd certainly given him enough reason to believe that about her—the house, all the stuff. All the things that she used to think could fill her up. She'd been such a stupid fool. It was a new way of thinking for her.

Selflessness. But who would have thought the first thing she'd let go would be the love of her life? Next would be all the stuff crowding her life. None of it mattered anymore.

Stin always knew when her heart was broken. The dog came and got in her lap. If she were human, Stin would cry with her, but this was as close as she could get.

"What am I supposed to do without him?" She sobbed tears that had long been held back. If only she didn't love Ryan so much, they could be together. If only she was willing to be selfish. But not this time.

She picked up the old Bible she'd found

hidden on a shelf in her closet, and let the Lord take her where he wanted her to go. The pages opened up to Psalm 30:5:

"Weeping endures for the night, but joy comes in the morning."

It would be a long night of weeping, but with the Lord on her side, she might be rewarded someday for letting the best thing in her life go.

Chapter 15

Vera had never made so much progress in such a short time. A for sale sign hung in her front yard, a small placard stating 'short sale' dangling right below.

Maggie, Amy, and Annie were helping her pack because she'd recently rented a small apartment in town two blocks from the cafe. Assistance with the deposit had come from, of all people, her mother. Not only would she have a short commute to work, but she could sell the car, too. The savings on gasoline and speeding tickets would be another huge boon.

She'd spoken to the foundation and rejected their offer of help, allowing all of it to go to Mrs. Jones. After all, Mrs. Jones was the victim of a swindle.

Vera had no real excuse because for years she'd overspent and overextended. It took coming back to the Lord to make her realize she didn't need any of the stuff that was suffocating her spirit, even her very soul.

"Where do you want this?" Amy held up a Tiffany lamp.

Her sister had come to town for the day to help out. For years, Amy had been the one to smooth over the tensions between Vera and their mother. Now, holiday dinners would be far less tense, and Amy had been grateful for the reconciliation, too.

"That's going to the foundation. They're raising money with an auction next week." They were getting anything she owned with a brand name attached to it as that would raise more money.

Annie sealed up a box and carried it to the truck.

Today was also the official moving day. While the realtor told Vera she could stay in the house until it sold, there was no time like the present to start her new life.

Thank the Lord for Jack and Maggie, who had agreed to allow Stin to live with them temporarily. Stin would still have a yard instead of being cooped up in the small apartment.

Vera would have liberal visitation rights, and it was a relief to know that Lexi would take good care of Stin until she left for college the following fall. Eventually Vera planned to rent a small home where she could have Stin with her again, and she had already started to save for it.

Most of what she owned would never fit in the small, one bedroom apartment so they would be driving her furniture over to foundation headquarters, and only a few essentials would be coming with her to her new place.

"I thought you'd be more disappointed than this." Amy packed the Tiffany lamp in a box.

There was a freedom in letting everything go— and a new hope Vera had in Christ. "I wish I'd figured it all out earlier. I don't need all this stuff."

"I'm proud of you." Amy grinned.

She hadn't seen Ryan since leaving her mother's home on the night of the concert, but even catching a glimpse of him in the cruiser as it passed through town called up piercing pain and a sob in her throat. She prayed that eventually it would get better, and maybe they could be friends again.

Maggie hadn't let up much in the past week.

"Have you seen Ryan lately?" Maggie now asked, as she wrapped a plate in newspaper and set it inside a cardboard box.

"Not for a while. I guess he goes to a different service time than I do."

"You know very well what service he goes to.

You're only trying to avoid him."

"Fine. I'm avoiding him."

"But why?"

"I need to do that for now." It was easier on her heart.

"You can't avoid him forever."

"Don't you think I know that? Just let me handle this my way. Sooner or later we'll be friends again." It was her hope and prayer, anyway.

"But I don't understand. Why aren't you two talking anymore? Can't you see you're perfect for each other?"

"We're not, Maggie. You're looking at things through your rose-colored glasses again. Take them off for a minute, would you?"

Behind them, Amy snorted. "Maybe you better put yours back on, Vera. I've seen Ryan. You need to think again. Annie and I will take this load over. See you in a bit."

"All I know is you must have said something to him. He loves you, and he wouldn't walk away that easily. What did you say to him?" Maggie pressed.

Vera was exhausted by the constant barrage of questions. Something told her that Maggie would get Ryan's side of the story, so after Amy and Annie left, she decided to tell Maggie the whole truth.

"You did what?" Maggie set down the box with a thud.

Fortunately, it contained nothing fragile.

"You heard me. I let him believe it because I knew he wouldn't try to talk me out of it. Call it male ego. Ryan has a healthy one, and he's proud of what he does."

"As well he should be." Maggie put her hands on her waist and glared at Vera.

"Don't look at me that way. You know I didn't mean it. Ryan and Jack—all of them —they're all heroes in my book."

"Then why would you hurt him like that?"

"You and I both know that if I told him the real reason he'd make up a million excuses. Better for him to be hurt a little now and get everything he deserves in the long run."

"You're scared that you can never have children.

That's what this is about, isn't it?"

"Almost a year of trying told me so."

"What about adoption? There are so many kids who need a home."

Apparently, Maggie was not going to let up on this. "That costs money, too. Lots of it."

"You surprise me." Maggie cocked her head to the side. "Why not be with the one you love and see what happens? Do you know how many married couples never know they'll encounter infertility? And yet somehow, they make it through."

"Some of them make it through. And others wind up hating each other, while they rack up a mountain of debt. I won't do that to Ryan. I won't do it to myself. I learned my lesson." She'd reasoned this all out in her bed every night, as she fought to find a way for them to be together. But there was just no way she'd shortchange Ryan's dream of having a family.

"OK, so let me see if I have this right. You're sacrificing your own happiness for his?"

"Something like that." Saying it that way sounded noble and that definitely wasn't her. She was a hurting mess. Dozens of times she'd picked up the phone and almost dialed his number because apparently she was a glutton for punishment.

"Oh, honey." Maggie looked at her with nothing but compassion in her green eyes. "What happened to the old Vera? The one who always got what she wanted?"

"She fell in love for the first time in her life. And more than anything else, I want him to be happy."

"But what if you're what he needs to be happy?"

Seven days of punishing workouts were not cutting it, but there was always today. Ryan ran a mile in five minutes and thirty seconds. Bench pressed his own weight, and hit the punching bag for thirty minutes. Nothing worked. He was still as angry as he'd ever been. And he still couldn't stop thinking about her.

Worse, as he prepared for his shift at the station, he knew he would get a lecture from Jack. He'd been a little over zealous yesterday with the teenage wanna- be hoodlums who liked to tag the huge fence that bordered the bookstore and faced Main Street—a blank canvas as far as they were concerned.

Sure enough, Jack waited for him, a grim expression on his face.

Ryan had to remind himself that Jack was his best friend, because right now he felt ready to box. "What's up?"

"You tell me. Something's going on with you, and I want to know what it is."

He ran a hand through his short cropped hair.

"You don't want to know."

"Sure I do. I want to hear it from you."

He folded his arms across his chest and leaned against his desk. "I don't make enough money for a certain woman."

"Is that right?" From behind his desk, Jack steepled his fingertips together.

"Yeah." He didn't exactly want to pour

his heart out to Jack. The anger was easier, and comfortable, like an old sweater.

"That never bothered you before."

"No one was ever quite so direct. And what burns me up the most is that I did everything right this time." He'd been the perfect gentleman. They were friends, and he'd fallen in love, hard, for the first time in his life.

"I would have to agree, but somewhere you lost your way."

"Come again?"

"You know I don't like repeating myself."

"What did you have in mind? Want me to quit and get a better job? Maybe as a banker? You know that'll never happen." Although for the first time in some time, he'd actually considered a return to competitive skiing. He'd have to travel, but he'd make a lot more money. Still, his pride got the best of him. He loved being a cop and too bad if it wasn't good enough for her.

"I think it's time to use deductive reasoning skills. I know we don't have many mysteries to solve in Harte's Peak, but here's one for you. Why would a woman turn you down because you don't make enough money and then give up almost everything she owns to start over again?"

"Vera was supposed to get help from the foundation. You mean she—"

"She turned it down and let Mrs. Jones have it all." He'd been out of touch, keeping to himself and licking his wounds. He figured Vera would deal with the foundation without him. Now he hit his desk with a fist. This was too much. Her stubbornness knew no bounds. "After all that effort."

"Did it ever occur to you that she realized that house was not what she wanted? She's been attending church, or haven't you noticed? And she is giving away most of her furnishings to the foundation for the auction."

This sounded like the Vera he thought he knew. The woman he'd fallen in love with, not the one who had dumped him due to his second-rate salary. He was completely confounded by women.

Jack rose from his desk, walked towards Ryan and clasped his shoulder with a firm hand. "I think you were outsmarted by Vera."

"I'm still confused."

Jack sighed. "She's got some crazy idea she's doing you a favor."

"By attacking my livelihood?"

"By letting you go. She's convinced herself that you deserve someone better. Someone without a past."

A light bulb flickered in his mind. He thought of Vera's miscarriage, her reluctance to hold baby John, and her insistence that some people weren't meant to have children. He'd told her in no uncertain terms that was what he wanted. Could that be what this was all about? "What does that mean? Doesn't she realize I have a past, too? And why not tell me the truth?"

"I don't know. I live with two women and I still can't give you the answer to that one. I think you'll have to come out and ask her," Jack said.

A new thought, almost too impossible to believe began to crowd his thoughts. Could it be that Vera loved him so much she would give him up? The crazy idea sounded like her way of thinking. "Jack—"

"Got you covered. I'll work some over time tonight. Maggie is at Vera's new apartment helping her get settled in. Here's the address." He handed a piece of paper to Ryan. "Don't be gone too long."

A girl's night was just what she needed, and Vera was happy that Maggie hadn't let her down. After Amy and Annie left, they sat on the couch surrounded by boxes, eating dark chocolate and painting their nails.

Maggie kept glancing at the clock.

"You don't have to stay much longer. I realize you're still nursing John." Vera didn't want Maggie to feel too sorry for her. The compassionate and sad glances in her direction were becoming too much. She felt sorry enough for herself and she didn't need anyone to reflect what she felt on the inside. It was easier to paste on a smile than to dwell in a constant state of tears.

"Lexi is giving him a bottle tonight for the first time. She's excited to do it, so don't worry. I can stay." Still, she kept her eye on the time as she blew on her fingernails.

Vera had unpacked the kitchen first and had cooked a homemade pizza for the two of them, a far cry from the one they'd ordered earlier.

"This is the best pizza I've ever had." Maggie bit into a second piece with gusto, exaggerating so obviously that Vera had to laugh. It was good to have friends.

"You don't have to do that."

"Do what?" Maggie widened her eyes.

"Try to constantly make me feel better: 'Why, Vera, this is the cutest dress I've ever seen. This is the best pizza I've ever tasted. Stin is the best behaved dog I've ever known.'" Vera smirked. "I'll be all right, you know."

"I know that." She put the slice down. "OK, sorry if I'm overdoing it."

"Just a tad," Vera said and rolled her eyes.

"So the truth is that Stin needs to get a handle on her hatred of all birds. What does she have against them?"

"There's a trick to it. Don't let her go outside every time she sees a bird. Distraction works. Offer her a biscuit, and she won't care if there is an entire bevy of birds outside."

"Lexi is having so much fun with her. She might even want to stay nearby for college because of Stin."

"You don't think her little brother might be enough to keep her nearby?"

"He's not as much fun as Stin."

"Tell her not to get too attached. I'll be out of this apartment in a few months." She had a plan, and she would stick to it.

Maggie smiled and looked at the clock again. "We might have to get Lexi a dog after you take Stin back."

A vehicle pulled up outside, its headlights shining into the tiny apartment.

Vera looked out the window.

Ryan emerged from the cruiser. He was still in his uniform, obviously on duty. What on earth was he doing here?

"It's Ryan." Vera turned to Maggie.

"Really?" Maggie stayed on the couch, strangely uninterested.

"What does he want?" Vera whispered as she moved toward the front door.

The man with the mocha eyes that haunted her dreams stood there.

She couldn't be expected to remain strong every minute, and her defenses were falling quickly. It was much easier not being around him. Why did he have to show up here tonight?

"I need to talk to you," Ryan said.

"Is something wrong? Is someone hurt?" Amy had left town on the long drive back hours ago. *Lord, please let my sister be safe.*

"No. Well, not exactly."

Vera turned at the sounds of Maggie gathering her purse, and rifling through it for her keys.

"Maggie wait, you don't have to——"

"Yes, I do." Maggie practically flew out the door without once looking back.

Great. She wondered how long Maggie and Jack had planned this. Leaving her here alone with Ryan raised the stakes in a way she'd never pictured them doing.

"That's funny." She gazed at Ryan. "She told me a few minutes ago she didn't have to go."

Ryan came inside.

She kept her distance. Being close to him was dangerous and habit inducing. She'd finally stopped aching enough to get through the day and now this. Surely, this would set her back and she could look forward to more tears tonight. "What is it?" She folded her arms across her chest like a shield over her heart.

"I'm feeling ambushed from all sides. I wonder how long Maggie planned this."

"I don't know, but I found out tonight." Ryan's eyes pierced her, a direct line to her heart.

"Found out what?"

"That you declined the foundation's help, that you're selling the house and all its contents. That you're starting over in this tiny apartment. Why didn't you tell me?"

"I was going to, eventually. I'm sure it would have come up in casual conversation."

"Why did you do it?" He took a step toward her.

"Before you get started on me, it's not because I thought I was undeserving."

"Good."

"I don't know if you can understand this, but I didn't want the house anymore. It was too much. I didn't need all those things. I have the Lord in my life again and I have peace about the next step in my life."

He cocked his head to the side. "Sounds like an awakening, all right. But when did you decide this?"

"I think it all happened the day of the concert." That night remained imprinted on her mind as the best night of her life. Star gazing on the hood of a car like a teenager. *Good grief.*

He took another step towards her.

She backed up a few steps to make up for the shrinking distance between them.

"Then why?"

"Ryan, do me a favor and stand over there, please." She pointed to a spot several feet away.

"What?" He looked at her with narrowed eyes.

"Why?"

"It's easier for me if you keep your distance." And also much better if he'd turn around and walk out that door before she changed her foolish mind.

"I see." He looked at the ground, and then stared into her eyes. "I'm not going to do that."

"Please." She couldn't be that strong anymore. Now that Ryan was before her, her mind played tricks while she reasoned that their relationship could work. Love would find a way. It might even be OK if they never had any children. But she'd decided not to be selfish anymore.

"Darlin', you have to tell me what's going on, because I won't leave here until you do."

Anger bubbled up inside her. Ryan was not playing fair.

"Why do you have to be so stubborn?"

"You're calling *me* stubborn? That's funny." He shook his head.

"You wouldn't give up until I told you about my baby." Her voice rose, and she had to remember that she now lived in a place where her neighbors might hear the slightest decibel increase.

"And that's what this is about, isn't it?"

He was forcing her to say it. Fine. "I saw your face when you were holding John. And you told me that's what you want—a family."

"So?"

"I can't give you that. I may never be able to have children. Why are you making me say this out loud? Don't you know how much it hurts?" Why couldn't he walk away and let her heal? Opening up the wounds and bleeding out would not help a thing.

He came even closer.

Backed up to the wall, she had nowhere left to go.

"The last thing I want to do is hurt you."

Now she stared into deep brown eyes so filled with warmth she couldn't breathe. Someone had taken all the oxygen out of the room.

"If you don't want to hurt me then why don't you step back, so I can…" Breathe? Think straight? All of the above.

"So you can do what?" He traced the curve of her face with his thumb.

"I don't know anymore." That's it. She'd lost the last brain cell she owned. Ryan's warm and simmering eyes probably melted it.

He drew her into his arms as she closed her eyes. Those arms were intoxicating and she breathed again, a deep sigh that reminded her of how much she'd missed being in the safety of his embrace. "Oh Ryan, what's the point?"

"The point is, I love you."

"I love you, too, but what if——"

He put his finger on her lips. "I don't care. Your love is the only love I need."

A peace surrounded her, a comfort she recognized.

"I want to believe that."

"Have I ever lied to you?"

"You say that now, but maybe someday you might change your mind."

"Can't you trust me? I love you."

"You already said that." She smiled.

"I'll keep saying it until you hear me. You're a stubborn woman."

"And you're a stubborn man."

He kissed her again, the way he'd done that night under the stars, his passion proving he would never give up on her. Somehow, together, and with God's help, they'd face whatever challenge lay ahead.

Epilogue

Six months later

The first annual Bachelor Auction of Harte's Peak was in full swing when Vera looked for a place among the crowded counter for her red velvet cake. She'd offered her café as the venue.

Ryan would meet her here, and since they both considered him to no longer be single, he'd volunteered to emcee the event.

He walked in dressed in a tuxedo. Surely, that was overkill. He'd managed to outshine the bachelors up for auction. She'd memorized the contours of his face and the way his thick dark hair felt running through her fingers, and her heart still made strange flips when he entered a room.

This time the group of bachelors included Tagg, the paramedic from county who, if the whispers of the women in attendance were any indication, would get the largest bid, and Lonnie Smith, the youngest deputy on the force. Although he still looked like a teenager, she'd been assured time and again he was twenty-five.

"Is that for me?" Ryan asked, seeing his favorite baked good. She'd now baked it three times for him in the six months they'd been dating. It was amazing how the man could eat.

"Tonight, you'll have to share it with the others." He frowned even though he must have known she'd bake it again the next evening if that made him happy.

Without a doubt, she was in love. Take her breath away, can't live without him, annoy everyone else in the room love. She must love him. She'd agreed to join him at the gym twice a week.

He claimed it was for her health and he wanted her to live a long time.

If nothing else, she hoped that proved her undying devotion to him.

They'd had to re-arrange the tables and chairs and create a small makeshift stage for the bachelors. But on this late September evening, the promise of autumn full in the air, the stringed white lights all along the stage and walls still created a wintry feeling.

She longed for the first snow fall.

Winter was now her favorite time of the year since a winter sport had brought them together. They'd be enjoying their first Christmas this year, and it was bound to be of special significance with her renewed faith.

Soon the auction would begin, and after that, she'd serve coffee and dessert to everyone, including the new couples who would proceed to plan the details of their date.

The proceeds would go to the Home is Where the Heart Is Foundation, Vera's new pet cause. She and Ryan devoted most of their spare time to the charity.

Ryan strode to the stage and made the introductions. But instead of beginning with Bachelor #1, Lonnie, eagerly waiting on the sidelines, Ryan asked her to come up and say a few words.

Fine. After all, she was officially the hostess.

She said a few words about the foundation, how many homes it had saved, and how many they planned to save. Then she thanked everyone for coming. As she prepared to leave the stage, Lexi walked up with Stin on a leash. Wrapped around Stin's middle was a canvas sack.

"Lexi? What's going on?" Vera asked.

Stin's tale wagged frantically, and she whined as she spotted Vera, but then the dog walked right past her to Ryan. Stin sat at his feet. *Traitor. One nice gorgeous guy comes around and you forget all about me.*

Vera glanced from Stin to Lexi, waiting for an explanation. When she turned to look at Ryan, the answer was clear.

Yes, he'd done it. It felt like a milestone achieved, like a victory he had to shout from the rooftops. Except no one else would understand. A few months ago at dinner with Vera's mother, he'd asked her for the framed photo of Vera, the one where she wore the royal blue gown and the look of innocence and joy. It was that smile he'd been working to put on her face since the day he'd told her he loved her.

He'd already seen it several times—once when he'd surprised her at Starlight Park with an evening picnic and they'd fallen asleep star gazing on the hood of his car in each other's arms. Tonight, though, was the culmination of all his plans, and as he dropped to his knees, he saw the look again. The look he hoped would never again leave her beautiful face.

He dug inside the sack tied around Stin for the boxed ring. The finest setting a public servant could afford. And fortunately, for him, the ring he'd seen Vera admiring many times in the past. He'd never done this before and couldn't believe he was about to do it now, and so publicly.

But as he glanced around, he saw the faces of his friends—so many friends, more than he ever deserved. Even Tagg and Lonnie grinned from ear to ear. Guys who never thought he'd settle down.

"Vera, I love you more than I have words to say. Right now, I wish I was a poet and not a cop because that's what you deserve. But if you'll have me, I would love for you to be my wife." He held the boxed ring in his shaking hands.

Vera laughed through tears. She tugged him up to a standing position and held his face in her hands. "I'd love to be your wife. I love you, Deputy. Even if you won't let me speed."

"She said yes!" Lexi shouted to the crowd, which erupted in spontaneous applause.

"Kiss! Kiss!" Jack began the chant until the café was filled with the sounds of their friends.

Nobody had to ask him twice. Ryan gazed into the blue eyes of his fiancée, eyes that reflected what he felt in his heart. He pulled her close, bent down and kissed her sweet lips. Not knowing what the future held for them—whether they would have children or not—felt like an adventure, not a death sentence.

He looked forward to waking up next to her every day for the rest of his life as they faced the uncertain future, their common faith a thread of gold that wove them together in the larger story of love and grace.

About the Author

Maria Michaels is a contemporary romance author who writes sweet, clean and wholesome books. The romances are still deeply emotional, but there's no bad language or sexual situations.

When early onset stage fright dashed dreams of Rock and Roll Hall of Fame status, Maria Michaels tackled her first novel in late 2010. She finished it in 2012, and now the fictional people that occupy her head refuse to leave.

She no longer sings unless you count randomly bursting into song to annoy her now adult children (and the dogs).

Maria lives in Northern California with her family.